An Encrypted Clue

Book 4 in ***The Math Kids*** *Series*

The Math Kids series

Have you read them all?

1. The Prime-Time Burglars

2. A Sequence of Events

3. An Unusual Pattern

An Encrypted Clue

*Book 4 in **The Math Kids** Series*

by

David Cole

Common Deer Press

Published by Common Deer Press Incorporated

Published in 2021 by Common Deer Press
3203-1 Scott Street
Toronto, Ontario
M5V 1A1

Library of Congress-in-Publication Data
Cole, David. – First edition
The Math Kids: An Encrypted Clue / David Cole
ISBN: 978-1-988761-56-5 (print)
ISBN: 978-1-988761-57-2 (e-book)

Cover Image: © Shannon O'Toole
Book Design: David Moratto
Printed in Canada

www.CommonDeerPress.com

To Rob, Bill, Laura, Linda, and Sarah.
Our family tree may not always have straight branches,
but there are some common roots in there somewhere.

Prologue

A loud crack of thunder startled me from a sound sleep. I had been dozing in the back of the car, but I was now fully awake. Sheets of rain pelted the car, and my father slowed the car to a crawl as the wipers struggled to keep up with the water streaming down the windshield.

"Wow, it's really coming down," I said.

"Well, at least we're almost home," my dad responded tersely. He concentrated on keeping the car centered in the road as he drove through the pouring rain.

I could barely make out the *Welcome to Maynard* sign as we crossed the town line. Lightning flashed, illuminating the hillside on the right of the two-lane highway. A winding road led up the hill, and as the rain lessened, I could just make out the dark mansion perched at the peak. As I continued to stare at the house, I thought I saw a wavering light in the middle window on the top floor. Another flash of lightning blinded me. When the darkness returned, I squinted through the rain, but the light was gone.

Chapter 1

Stephanie Lewis squinted at the tiny handwriting in the margin of the book. At first, it looked like someone had just been doodling. When she put her nose almost to the page, however, she could just make out the tiny writing.

The strange symbols didn't mean anything to her, but she carefully copied them into her notebook anyway.

Stephanie had spent the afternoon at the library working on a social studies project. Her family had moved into the area at the beginning of the school year, so the project to track the history of Maynard was helping her to learn about her new town. The paper only had to be three pages long, but Stephanie had already collected almost seven pages of notes. The latest book she was studying, A *Short History of Maynard*, was anything but short. It was almost four hundred pages long. It was on page 213 that Stephanie found the cryptic note.

Maynard, like most small towns anywhere, doesn't really have enough history to fill four hundred pages, but it still has enough stories to be interesting. It was founded in 1874 by Herbert Maynard. Herbert was the first mayor of the town, which in the beginning consisted primarily of other Maynards. The extended family had made its living mining the veins of rich black coal from the caves just north of town. By the early 1900s, the town had grown to almost a thousand people, and Herbert Maynard had grown very wealthy. He built a sprawling mansion on the tallest hill overlooking the town and less than a football field from the entrance to the caves that had given his family, and the town, its start. But he only got to enjoy two short years in his new home as he and his wife, Olivia, were struck down with yellow fever in 1904 and died just days apart in their master bedroom. They were not to be the only ones to die in the mansion.

After Herbert's death, his sons, Urban and Eustis Maynard, took over the mining operation, but it wasn't long before disaster struck. A landslide in 1908 buried almost a dozen miners, and the brothers were forced to seal off the cave system. With the closing of the coal mine, most of the men in town were suddenly unemployed, but Urban and Eustis started Maynard Manufacturing and quickly put everyone back to work. The company prospered making canvas tents,

farming tools, and buggy parts. The invention of the automobile eventually forced them out of the buggy business, but by then World War I had kicked into full gear and the brothers made a small fortune selling helmets and ammunition to the army. When the war ended, Maynard Manufacturing employed almost half of the residents of the growing town. Urban remained single, but Eustis married, and he and his wife, Martha, had a son named Douglas in 1916. The four lived a luxurious life in the family mansion, their every need promptly tended to by a staff of cooks, butlers, and housemaids.

While the Depression of the 1930's hit the country hard, Maynard Manufacturing kept their doors open and the town employed. It was said that the Maynard family lost a fortune in the stock market, but it didn't seem to faze them. They continued to live the life of royalty.

While they remained wealthy, bad luck continued to follow them. Urban was electrocuted when he was trying to repair a faulty light switch in the basement of the mansion. Eustis died four years later when he tripped and fell down the main staircase. Douglas married and had a son, Cletus, in 1940, but his wife died during childbirth. In 1958, Douglas died on Christmas Eve when he fell off a ladder while placing the angel on top of the Christmas tree.

That left the eighteen-year-old Cletus as the last remaining member of the Maynard family. He went to college and earned a degree in history. He married his college sweetheart and returned to the mansion.

In 1965, Cletus's wife, Elenore, came down with a bad case of pneumonia. For days, Cletus sat by her side as she grew steadily weaker. The only doctor in town tried everything he knew to cure her, but she died early on a Saturday morning. Cletus made the long walk into town that afternoon. After planning for his wife's funeral and burial, he returned to his house on the hill. He was never seen again.

More than fifty years later, the Maynard mansion still stands on top of the hill, but no one from the Maynard family lives there. The town now owns it and operates it as a museum. Busloads of kids still visit the Maynard House on field trips to learn about the town's history. Since this is usually done in third grade and she hadn't moved to town until fourth, Stephanie had never been there. She bet her friends Justin, Jordan, and Catherine had all been there though. She would have to remember to ask them during the next meeting of the Math Kids.

The Math Kids began as a club to solve math problems. Stephanie and her friends were all in the highest math group in their class and loved to work on difficult problems. And they were pretty good at it too! They had won the fourth-grade math competition at McNair Elementary last month and would compete against the other schools in town in the spring.

The Math Kids had used their math skills to solve some other tricky problems too, including tracking down a kidnapper, figuring out a fifteen-year-old bank robbery, and even capturing some burglars trying to rob Stephanie's house.

Stephanie squinted again at the tiny handwriting in the margin of the book. What did the strange symbols mean?

Could this be another case for the Math Kids?

Chapter 2

My name is Jordan Waters, and I'm the president of the Math Kids club. There are only four of us in the club—me, Justin Grant, Stephanie Lewis, and Catherine Duchesne. I was appointed president since the club was originally my idea, but my title doesn't really mean anything. We are all equal partners in everything we do, and we are proof of the old saying that "the whole is greater than the sum of its parts." We are all pretty good at solving problems by ourselves, but our team is fantastic when we solve them together.

"Here's what I found," Stephanie said excitedly as she wrote the symbols onto the whiteboard in Justin's basement. "You think it means anything?"

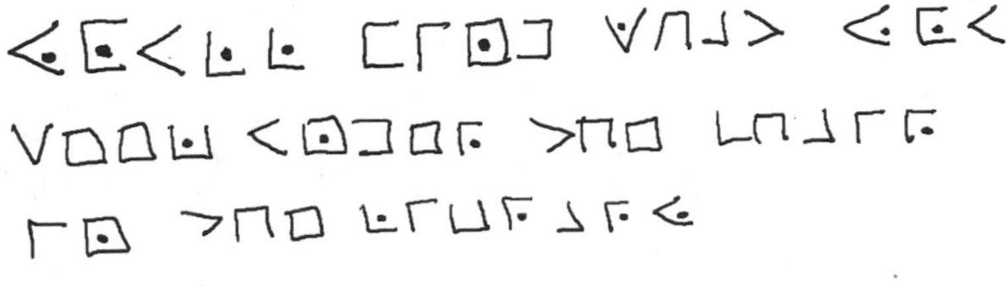

Justin stared at the symbols and smiled. He quickly scribbled something onto a sheet of paper and then stood in front of the board. He glanced back and forth between his paper and the symbols, nodding the entire time.

"It's a pigpen cipher," he said. "Don't you remember Mr. Wynkoop teaching us that in Cub Scouts, Jordan?"

In a flash, it came back to me. Our cubmaster had taught us a simple cipher. Justin and I had used it one whole summer to send secret messages back and forth to each other.

"It's pretty simple," Justin explained as he drew on the whiteboard.

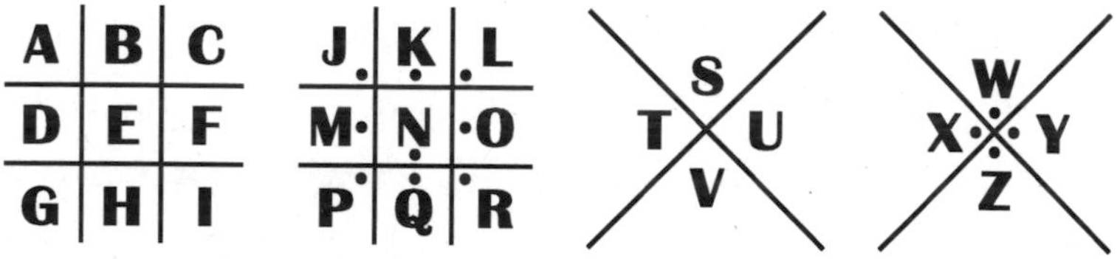

"Each letter is represented by the shape it's in," Justin said. "Since the *E* is in a square, it would be shown as a square in the cipher. The *B* would be shown as a square with no top. The *S* would look like a *V*, and so on. If a shape has a dot in it, the symbol will also show a dot."

"That's a pretty cool code," Catherine said.

"Actually, it's a cipher," Justin corrected her. "A cipher

substitutes one character or symbol for another. *A* might mean *N*, *B* means *O*, and so on."

"So, what's a code then?" Stephanie asked.

"In a code, the word *dog* might mean 'attack in the morning.' The difference is that someone can figure out a cipher, but with a code there's no way to understand the message unless you get your hands on the codebook."

We looked again at the message Stephanie had copied out of the margin in the book.

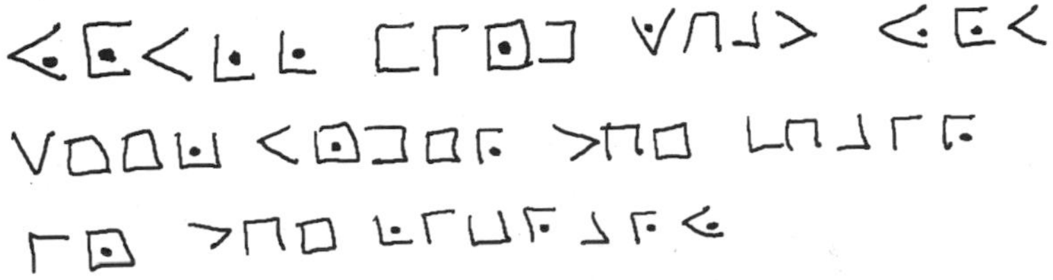

We compared it to the key Justin had drawn on the board.

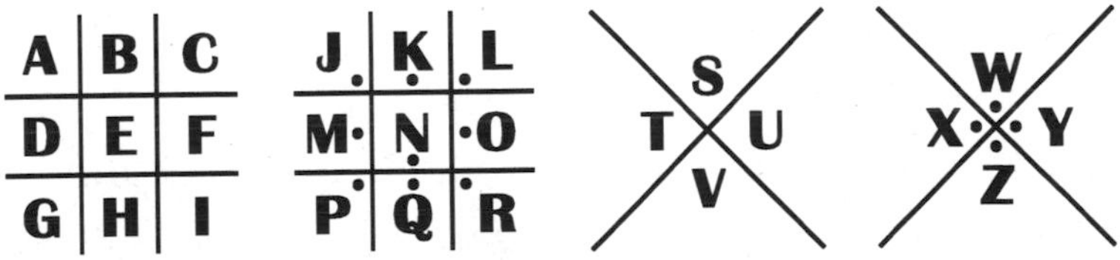

We checked each symbol in the message, and in a couple of minutes, we had a solution.

You'll find what you seek under the chair in the library

We high-fived each other for solving the mystery of the symbols, but Stephanie had a frown on her face.

"What's wrong, Stephanie?" Catherine asked.

"Great, we solved the code…" she started.

"Cipher," Justin correct.

"Fine, we solved the cipher," she said snippily, drawing a frown from Justin, "but now what? What is it we're supposed to be seeking?"

"Here's another problem," I added. "There are hundreds of chairs in the library. Are we supposed to check every single one until we find something?"

"And what if someone is just messing with us?" Catherine added.

"But what if they aren't?" Justin asked. "I think somebody left that message for someone to find."

"We need to figure out who left the message," Stephanie said. "Looks like I'm headed back to the library."

"Not without us, you're not!" I said.

Two hours later, we had looked under almost every chair in the library. I say almost because there were people sitting in some of them. An elderly man with a long gray beard was dozing in one while Mrs. Carmichael, our school librarian, was firmly planted in another. She looked like she was settled in for the day with a stack of old magazines on the table in front of her.

"You'd think after working in a library all week that another library would be the last place someone would want to be," Stephanie pointed out.

"I don't know," Catherine countered. "My dad teaches math all week and does math at home all weekend."

"But that's different," Justin protested. "That's math!"

"Well, this was kind of a bust," I said. "All I managed to find was old gum."

"Yuck," said Stephanie.

"Yeah, it doesn't have much flavor left," I said as I pretended to chew.

"That's gross!" Stephanie groaned.

"I wish we had some idea of when the message was written," Catherine said.

"Why?" I asked.

"Well, if the message was written a long time ago, these might not even be the same chairs."

"I didn't think of that."

"Maybe we should ask the librarian," Stephanie suggested. "They should have a record of who has checked out the book."

Unfortunately, the librarian told us she was not allowed to give out information on who had checked out books. After seeing the looks on our faces though, she reconsidered.

"Let me pull it up on the computer," she said. "At least I can tell you *when* it was last checked out."

She typed some information on the keyboard, clicked the mouse a few times, and then shook her head. "I'm sorry kids, but it looks like no one has ever checked that book out."

"Ever?" Stephanie said.

"Well, at least not since 1997 when we computerized all of the checkouts," she replied.

"How were checkouts done before that?" Justin asked.

She smiled. "It was pretty old-fashioned," she said. "You signed and dated the card for the book. We kept the card until the book was returned, and then we'd return the card to the pocket glued to the inside of the back cover."

We thanked the librarian and walked to one of the wooden tables. We held our breath as Stephanie opened the back cover of the book. There it was. The yellowed cardstock pocket was still attached. Stephanie yanked the checkout card from the pocket.

The checkout information was written in a shaky script, but they could still make out the last checkout date of September 23, 1984. The name next to the date was Cletus Maynard.

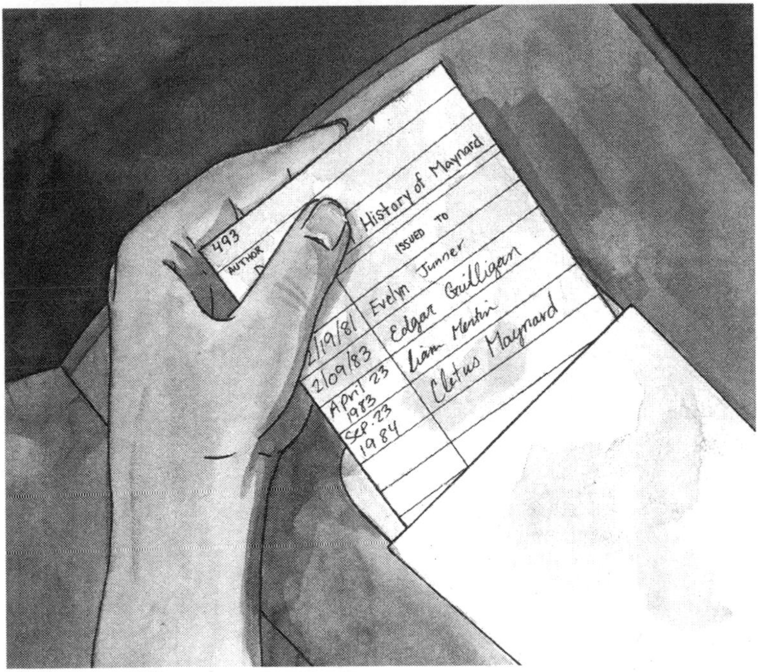

"But that can't be right!" Stephanie protested. "Cletus Maynard disappeared in 1965. How can he have checked out this book nineteen years later?"

It didn't make any sense. When Cletus's wife, Elenore, had died, no one had ever seen Cletus again. Or had they?

"And even if it was Cletus, can we be sure that it was him who wrote in the book?" Stephanie asked.

"I'm afraid I've got bad news," Justin said.

We all looked at him, dreading the worst. And, unfortunately, Justin delivered exactly that.

"This library was built in 1988," he said. "The old

library was torn down in 1990 to put up the Southside mini-mall. And, before you ask, they bought all new furniture when they built the new library."

So that was it. It didn't matter that we had solved the puzzle. The old library was gone. Even if Cletus—or someone else—had hidden something under one of the chairs, it was gone now. We were at a dead end.

Stephanie, Catherine, and I sat silently around the table. There was a cloud of defeat hanging over us. I looked around for Justin. He had wandered off and I didn't see him at first, but then spotted him on the other side of the library. I watched as he walked down the row of windows, reversed direction as he reached the far wall, and then followed the row of windows again. A small smile broke over my face as I realized what he was doing.

Justin and I had been best friends since kindergarten, so I knew what was happening. When he was thinking hard about a problem, he tuned everything else out and went into what he called "the zone." He became so engrossed in solving the problem that he often lost all track of where he was or what he was doing. Luckily, this time he was in a closed room. Once, he had wandered almost a mile away before he looked up to find out he was lost. The good thing was that when Justin came out of the zone, he usually brought an answer with him. I wasn't expecting that to happen this time though. There was nothing in the zone that was going to bring a library chair back from a pile of rubble.

Justin stopped in the middle of the wall of windows. He stood perfectly still for almost a minute, then looked up like he wasn't sure where he was. A sly grin came across his face, and he was still smiling when he returned to the table.

"What if there *is* another library?" he asked.

Chapter 3

Four days later, Justin had still not told us what he meant when he asked if there could be another library. It was driving Catherine and Stephanie crazy, but I had known Justin long enough to know that we would just have to wait until he was good and ready to tell us. I remember one time in November he told me he had come up with the perfect Halloween costume. Even though I had tried to get it out of him for months, he made me wait until the following Halloween when he finally unveiled the costume—a giant Rubik's Cube with sides that could really move.

While we waited for Justin to spill the beans on his library idea, Mrs. Gouche, our teacher, was working hard to get us ready for the district math contest at the end of the school year. The four of us were in the yellow group, which was the top math group in our class. The Math Kids had won against the other fourth-grade classes at our school, beating Joe Christian's team on the last question. We had Catherine and her favorite number, 55, to thank for that!

This week we were working on problems having to do with using balance scales. "Okay, here's the problem for today," Mrs. Gouche began. "Someone tried to pay you with twelve gold coins. You learned that one of the coins is fake. It looks identical, but it's just a little heavier than the others. You have a balance scale. Can you find the fake coin using the scale only three times?"

Wait! Do you want to try to solve this puzzle before seeing if the Math Kids can do it? Using the balance scale only three times, can you figure out which of the twelve coins is heavier than the others? Here's one important hint for you: once you find out a coin is real, you can use that coin to tell if another coin is heavy. Good luck!

Mrs. Gouche left to work with the other math groups, so we huddled together at the whiteboard in the front of the room. We had been working with weighing problems like this all week, so we had learned some lessons about approaching the problem.

"Let's start by putting four coins on each side and

leave the other four on the side," I suggested. "Then we'll be able to narrow down the bad coin to one of four coins."

One thing we had learned was that sometimes it was easier to solve a problem if we could visualize it, so Stephanie went to the board to keep track of our moves. We decided to use a *G* if we knew a coin was good and a question mark if we weren't sure.

Weighing 1

Weighing 1 Potential Result A (scales balance)

Weighing 1 Potential Result B (scales don't balance)

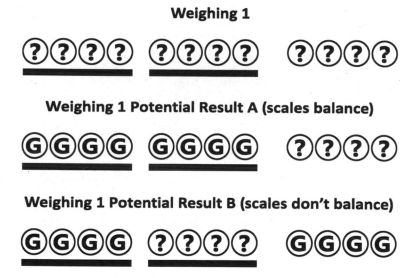

Stephanie wrote down the possible outcomes of the first weighing. If the two scales balanced, that meant the bad coin was one of the four we hadn't weighed yet. Otherwise, the bad coin was on whichever side of the scale that was heaviest.

"Okay, we're down to four coins," Catherine asked.

"We could put two of the unknown coins on each side and see which side is heavier. Then, on the third weighing we can weigh those two and see which one is heavier."

Stephanie thought about this for a moment and then said, "I think there's another way." She drew her thoughts on the board.

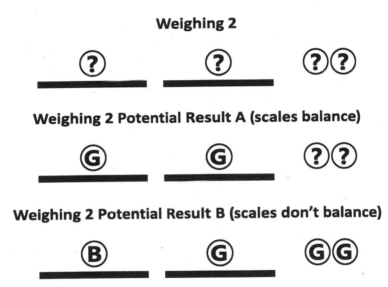

Weighing 2

Weighing 2 Potential Result A (scales balance)

Weighing 2 Potential Result B (scales don't balance)

Justin nodded in agreement. "Yeah, if the scales don't balance, we know right away which one is the bad coin and we wouldn't even need a third weighing. At the worst, we're down to two coins and can easily figure out which one of those is heaviest."

Stephanie drew the third weighing to complete the problem.

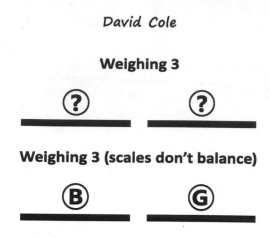

Weighing 3

Weighing 3 (scales don't balance)

"Way to go, team!" Justin yelled, causing Mrs. Gouche to frown from the back of the room where she was working with the red math group. She liked that we were enthusiastic about working on difficult math problems, but she wasn't always happy about our volume when we solved one. She rose from her chair and came to the whiteboard to check our work.

"That looks correct," she said.

Justin looked a little irritated that she had doubted us, even a little. "You sound surprised," he said, sounding somewhat hurt.

"Oh, I had no doubt you could do this one," she said, smiling at Justin. "But I wonder if you could do the same problem if you didn't know if the coin was heavier or lighter." With that, she walked back to the red math group and their struggles with long division.

"That doesn't seem like it would be much harder," I said.

But I was very wrong. We finally got it, but it was weeks later, and a whole lot of interesting things happened to us in the meantime.

If you want to see how the Math Kids solved this puzzle, check out the appendix at the back of the book. But first, try to solve it yourself! Using the balance scale only three times, can you figure out which of the twelve coins has a different weight (heavier or lighter) than the others?

Chapter 4

That weekend, Justin came to the meeting of the Math Kids bearing a stack of books. He had done that before, but usually they were books of math puzzles. There was nothing we loved better than solving tough problems using math. This time, though, he brought history and geography books about Maynard and the surrounding area. I thumbed through one called *The Caves of Northern Virginia*.

"I've already looked through most of these," Stephanie said as she looked through the other books.

"That's what I figured," Justin replied, "but did you come across this one?"

He held up a dusty book with a leather cover. We gathered around to look at the title, *Historic Libraries of North America*.

"I was looking at the history of Maynard, not the history of libraries," Stephanie responded.

"I know, but I found something interesting that may help solve our problem," Justin said. "Check this out.

The oldest library system in America was started with a donation of four hundred books from a clergyman named John Harvard. Yep, the same guy that Harvard University is named after. Do you know that the Harvard library now has more than twenty million books?"

Stephanie started, "That's really interesting, Justin, but—"

Justin continued like he hadn't even heard her. "When the British burned down the Library of Congress during the war of 1812, the Americans restarted the library by buying Thomas Jefferson's collection of more than six thousand books. Now it has more than thirty-nine million books."

We all looked at the illustration of the Library of Congress on fire. Again, interesting, but where was Justin going with this?

"And between 1881 and 1919," he continued, "Andrew Carnegie helped build more than one thousand seven hundred public libraries across the United States."

When Justin finally came up for a breath of air, I jumped in. "That's all cool, Justin, but what does that have to do with the clue Stephanie found?"

"Everything," he said triumphantly. He opened the book to a page marked with a sticky note and read.

In 1891 Maynard, Virginia, opened its first public

library when Herbert Maynard, the founder and mayor of the small mining town, bequeathed 1,250 books and donated money for a building in which they could be housed.

"And you think that might be the library that the clue was talking about?" Stephanie asked excitedly.

"I did, but it turns out the first Maynard library was hit by lightning in 1914 and burned to the ground," he said.

"Was there anything left from the fire?" Catherine asked.

"Nothing left but ashes."

"Then why did you even bring it up?" I asked grumpily. "I thought you said you had something that would solve our problem. It sounds like just another dead end to me."

"Maybe," Justin said, "but then again, maybe not."

We all looked at him, waiting for him to go on, but he just sat there with a wide grin on his face. We waited him out, and finally he continued.

"Stephanie, you weren't here yet, but Jordan and Catherine probably remember taking a field trip to the old Maynard House," he said.

Catherine and I nodded our heads.

"And you remember that some of the rooms were roped off, so we couldn't go in, right?"

"Yeah," I said. "I know they wouldn't let us go in the basement, the master bedroom, and—"

"The library!" Catherine finished with a yell.

And then I remembered. The room was large, with a gigantic fireplace at one end and wall to wall books everywhere else. The woodwork and bookshelves were darkly stained walnut, and there were thick velvet curtains covering the beautiful stained-glass windows. Beautiful crystal chandeliers provided light over the overstuffed armchairs and reading tables. I remember thinking it was one of the most beautiful rooms I had ever seen.

"And do you remember why they said we couldn't go in those rooms?" Justin asked.

I did remember, and now I knew where Justin was going with this. I silently high-fived him.

"What am I missing?" Stephanie asked.

Catherine also looked confused.

"They wouldn't let us in the rooms because they still had the original furniture in them," Justin said.

Of course! Before there was a Maynard Public Library, there had been a Maynard private library, and that building was still in pristine shape with the original furniture still sitting there, just waiting to spill its secrets.

"How do we get in to check out the chairs?" I asked.

"I have a plan for that," Justin answered.

That didn't surprise me a bit. After all, coming up with plans is what Justin does best. It was his plan that helped us catch the burglars (with a little help from Stephanie and Robbie Colson's dad). It was Justin's plan for us to gather evidence on the men who had kidnapped Catherine's dad, and it was his plan to get Phil Duke to confess to framing Old Mike, the school janitor. Like I said, planning is what Justin does best.

"It's not something crazy, is it?" I asked.

"Nothing crazier than usual," he said with a smile.

"Why is that not very comforting?" I asked.

"Seriously, nothing crazy. I just think it's time for Stephanie to get her first visit to the old Maynard House," he said innocently.

I breathed a sigh of relief. I mean, how much trouble could we get into visiting an old house?

Once again, I turned out to be very wrong.

Chapter 5

The next Saturday, Justin's mom drove the four of us to the old Maynard mansion.

"Didn't you already come here on a field trip last year?" she asked.

"Um, yeah, but Stephanie wasn't here, so we decided to show her about the history of Maynard," Justin replied.

"Well, that's awfully nice," she said as she pulled into the circular drive in front of the house. She had to wait at the entrance as an elderly man with a gray beard and ancient overcoat made his way slowly through the crosswalk. He glanced over at us as our car drove past him. Something about the man was familiar, but I couldn't put my finger on it, and I quickly put it out of my head when Justin's mom brought the car to a halt.

"I'll pick you up at four," she said.

We hopped out of the car and headed toward the house, but when we looked around, Stephanie wasn't with us. I looked back, and she was standing at the curbside, staring at the old house.

"You coming with us, Stephanie?" I asked.

"Um, yeah, I guess," she said.

"What's up?" Catherine asked.

"Well, it's just that…just that…"

"Let me guess. Someone told you it was haunted, didn't they?"

Stephanie nodded sheepishly. "I mean, there were a lot of people who died in this house," she said, tugging nervously at her ponytail.

"Yeah, but that doesn't mean they're floating around and rattling chains," Justin said.

"Some people say that they have heard bumping sounds from behind the walls when they took the tour," Catherine countered.

"That's just their imagination running away with them," Justin said.

"And our tour guide told us they sometimes found the furniture moved in the library," Catherine said.

"He was probably just trying to drum up business," Justin scoffed. "The more people who think it's haunted, the more people will visit. I don't believe him or the people who say they've seen lights in the windows at night."

I didn't say anything. I was thinking back to that rainy night when I thought I had seen a light. I looked up at the second floor, trying to figure out which window it had been.

"So, are we doing this or not?" Justin asked. "We've all heard the stories, Stephanie, but I promise you that's all they are—stories."

Stephanie gave a nervous giggle.

"Of course," she replied. "I know that." She sounded a little unsure, but she followed us to the front door.

It was two dollars for adults to tour the mansion, but it was only a dollar for kids. We paid and waited on the front porch for the next tour to start. The weather was starting to get chilly, and we were shivering by the time we were finally able to enter the house.

Stephanie gasped as she entered the door into the grand foyer. An enormous chandelier hanging from the thirty-foot tall ceiling shone brightly with hundreds of lights. The large room was flanked on both sides by a curving staircase rising to the second floor. A large doorway opened to a dining room on one side of the foyer. The other side opened to a formal living room with enough seating for dozens of people.

"Wow, this place is amazing," Stephanie said in a loud whisper.

"I forgot how big it was," Catherine agreed.

"See that oil painting on the wall over there?" I asked, pointing to a large picture with an enormous gold leaf frame. "That's Cletus and Elenore Maynard."

The painting showed a young, handsome man in a dark blue suit. His arm was around a pretty, blonde woman in a flattering green dress. Both displayed broad smiles, like they were laughing at a joke the painter had made.

Stephanie started to say something about the picture but was interrupted by the booming voice of the tour guide.

"Welcome to the Maynard House," he said. "The original house was built in 1903 by Herbert Maynard, the founder and first mayor of Maynard. The east wing was added by his sons, Urban and Eustis, in 1909."

He went on to explain the story of the Maynard family and the tragic deaths that had occurred in the mansion. He finished his introduction with Elenore's death and Cletus's disappearance.

"With no known remaining heir," our tour guide concluded, "the town of Maynard took possession of the house and all of the surrounding land. So, who's ready to see the house?"

There were ten people in our tour group. We had been hoping for more, but we were going to have to make do with what we had. The guide led us through the dining room, the butler's pantry, and the kitchen, which was bigger than that of most restaurants. We saw elaborately decorated bedrooms, the music room with a pair of Fazioli Brunei grand concert pianos decorated with semiprecious stones, and a ballroom that could easily hold a hundred people. We finally arrived at the door leading to the library. The doorway was blocked by a velvet rope strung between two polished brass poles.

"I'm sorry we can't go into the library, but it still holds the original furniture and rugs, so we want to protect them," the guide said.

We looked at each other and nodded. That means the original chairs. Were they the ones referred to in the clue Stephanie found? It was time to put Justin's plan into action.

"Herbert Maynard started the first public library in town by donating two thousand books," our guide went on.

"One thousand two hundred and fifty," Justin corrected. I coughed quietly.

"No, it was two thousand," the guide insisted.

"It was one thousand two hundred and fifty," Justin said stubbornly. I coughed a little louder.

"I've been giving this tour for more than four years, and I can assure you that Mr. Maynard donated two thousand books," the guide said, just as stubbornly.

"It was one thousand two hundred and fifty, and I can prove it," Justin countered. I elbowed him sharply.

"Ow!" he said. "What was that for?"

That's when he got it. Justin was supposed to quietly sneak into the library after the tour had moved on. Instead, his stubbornness had drawn the tour guide's attention to him. There was no way he would be able to slip away now. The guide would be paying attention to him.

Across the hallway, I could see Stephanie look in my direction.

"Plan B," she mouthed silently to me. I nodded.

The tour guide motioned us down the hallway in the direction we had come. In the commotion of getting the group turned around, Stephanie slipped under the rope and into the library.

I thought we were home free until I heard a small clunking sound from the library. I thought maybe the guide hadn't heard it, but then he turned back toward the room.

"Please wait here. I'll be back shortly," he told the group.

When he reached the doorway to the library, I held my breath. He scanned the room, looking for anything out of place. He took a step back down the hallway, then paused, listening carefully. There was silence except for the quiet murmuring of the tour group down the hallway. Still not satisfied, he returned to the library doorway and moved the brass pole holding up one side of the rope and stepped into the room.

From my vantage point, I could see into the library. Nothing looked out of place at first, but then I saw it. Just peeking out from beneath one of the heavy curtains was the tip of a white sneaker. The guide was only steps away from Stephanie's hiding place. If he moved the curtain, she would be caught! He raised his hand toward the curtain.

"Excuse me," I said loudly, startling the guide.

"What is it?" he asked sharply.

"I had some questions about the…about the…" I stammered.

"Please wait with the rest of the group," he said. "I'll be out in a second." He turned back to the curtain.

I decided to go with my own Plan B. "Where's the bathroom?" I asked.

The guide paused with his hand on the curtain.

"It's kind of an emergency," I said. "I think I might throw up." I made retching sounds as I leaned over the expensive-looking rug just inside the library doorway.

The gagging noise got his attention and he ran quickly across the room. "Not on the rug!" he said urgently. He rushed me down the corridor to a room marked *Men*. I went in the room and locked the door behind me. I had to fight back nervous giggles as I thought about how close he had come to discovering

Stephanie hiding behind the curtain. I wanted to buy Stephanie some time, so I ran the tap for a while before leaving the restroom.

The guide looked at me anxiously as I came out of the room.

"Is everything okay?" he asked.

"I feel much better, thanks," I said. I could see him breathe a sigh of relief.

The rest of the tour went on without the guide noticing that Stephanie was no longer in the group. When the tour was over, we were escorted out of the mansion. The rest of our group moved toward their cars, but Catherine, Justin, and I remained on the porch. We all had the same thought running through our heads. Stephanie had made it into the library, but how was she going to get back out?

Forty minutes passed with no sign of our friend. Finally, the front door opened, and the next tour group began to exit. Trailing just behind the group was Stephanie! She was talking animatedly to an older woman wearing floral pants and a bright yellow sweatshirt.

"Wasn't that a great tour, Grandma?" Stephanie gushed.

"But, I'm not your grandma," the woman replied in confusion.

By then, the group had cleared the door and Stephanie turned and gave the woman a smile. “Oh, I’m sorry, I thought you were someone else,” she said sweetly.

She hurried over to where we were huddled by a bench.

“Did you find it?” I whispered.

Stephanie held up her phone. “It’s all right here,” she said.

The Math Kids high-fived each other. We had pulled it off!

The woman in the floral pants looked over at us, but the rest of the tour group walked away without paying us any attention.

Chapter 6

On Sunday, Stephanie went to her cousin's birthday party, which turned out to be an all-day event, so we couldn't see what she had discovered in the old library. We decided to meet after class on Monday, but an unexpected announcement changed that plan.

Mrs. Gouche told us there was going to be an assembly at ten in the morning. We weren't very happy about that because it was right in the middle of our math time. The halls were crowded with students headed to the gym. When we arrived, the large room was packed with students sitting in the bleachers. I was surprised to see that parents had also been invited. My mom waved to me from her folding chair on the floor of the gym. Stephanie's parents were both there, as was Catherine's dad, who was a math professor at the college. I didn't see Justin's parents, but I may have just missed them in the large crowd.

Mrs. Arnold, the principal, went to the podium

set up at one end of the gym. There were two men seated on chairs near the podium. They were wearing dark suits and had grim looks on their faces.

"Thank you for coming on such short notice," Mrs. Arnold started. She waited a few seconds for the crowd to settle down. "I'm Mrs. Arnold, the principal here at McNair Elementary. I'm joined this morning by Walter Evans, the Maynard comptroller, and Tony King, the president of the board of education. They will be sharing some important information with you this morning."

Mr. Evans took the microphone in one hand and looked out at the crowd. The look on his face told me the news wasn't going to be something we wanted to hear.

"Thank you, Mrs. Arnold. Thank you, parents, for your participation today. And thank you students, for taking time from your morning schedule. I'm afraid the news I'm going to share is not great."

There was a murmur throughout the crowd. Mr. Evans waited for the crowd to settle down, then raised the microphone once again.

"As many of you probably already know, the city of Maynard is facing a financial crisis due to a sharp reduction in our tax base for the previous two years. Lack of funding is forcing us to make some tough choices over the next twelve months. And, as is unfortunately too often the case, these choices will have a negative impact on the school district."

The murmuring grew louder.

Mr. Evans held his hand up to quiet the crowd. He handed the microphone to Mr. King.

"We understand that any cuts to the school budget are painful. We're working very closely with Mr. Evans and the rest of the town council to minimize the impact of any cuts. I've been in meetings with the rest of the school board, principals from each of the schools, as well as a team of teachers, to review our recommendations for cuts."

The murmuring from the crowd had now turned into angry shouts.

"What kind of cuts?"

"How will this affect my kids?"

"Why can't we trim somewhere else?"

Even with the microphone, Mr. King had to shout to be heard over the crowd. "Please hear us out, folks. My own kids went to McNair and are now at the high school, so my own family will be affected too. We are doing the best we can to stretch the budget, but cuts will have to be made. Here is the list of cost reductions we are recommending."

He tapped a few keys on the laptop sitting on the podium, and a large screen behind him projected the school board recommendations.

The crowd quieted for a few minutes as they read through the list.

I scanned the list myself and stopped when I reached one item.

23. *Eliminate district-wide math and science competitions.*

The next hour went by in a blur. Mr. King tried to defend the cuts against a parade of angry people voicing their opinions. There were teachers angrily denouncing the freeze in salaries. There were parents protesting cuts in different programs. It seemed everyone had something they wanted to defend, whether it was the high school marching band, a sports team, the computer lab, or some other program I had never even heard of. Who even knew that there was money going to maintain a nature trail behind the middle school?

Throughout the long hour, all I could think about was that we weren't going to be able to represent our school in the spring math competition, which was now only a month away. It just wasn't fair. We had trained too hard to have that taken away from us!

Chapter 7

It was two more days before the Math Kids had a chance to see what Stephanie had found in the library at the old Maynard House. We met at Catherine's house this time. Stephanie had printed a copy of the image she had taken with her phone. We stood around the table in Catherine's living room and stared at the single sheet of paper.

FURAF	*TSGAT*	*FQTQY*	*UFKDQ*	*HQTSG*	*MXDQT*
FMRPZ	*MDSKY*	*QPMYF*	*MTFQO*	*MXBMZ*	*UZQPP*
UTEUT	*FMBQG*	*DFQTF*	*ZAUFM*	*ZUFEQ*	*PQTFT*
OMQDG	*AKQDA*	*RQNPQ*	*WOAXN*	*QNXXU*	*IKQZD*
GAVDG	*AKFGN*	*WQQEG*	*AKDQN*	*YGZQT*	*FEUQZ*
UZ-KFZ	*QHQEE*	*OUFUX*	*ABIAX*	*XARFA*	*ZAPAT*
IQEAT	*FDARP*	*QZUMS*	*DQTFM*	*RPZMD*	*SKYIA*
TEUFE	*AXQTI*	*ATPQQ*	*ZPXGA*	*IGAKE*	*QGXOQ*
TFXXM	*QPUHA*	*DBPXG*	*AIQDG*	*XUMRX*	*MUFZQ*
PUEQD	*BMPQX*	*MQHQD*	*FEDUR*	*EMIFU*	*TOUTI*

YADRE EQZWD MPQTF KNPQD QHAOQ DFGNP
ZGARE MIFUQ DQTIE ZUMYQ DQDGE MQDFQ
TFFZQ DQRRU PKXQD UFZQS ZUTFQ YAEEP
XQUKW QQEQI FMTIE QYUFQ YAEED MQBBM
FUEME KMIXM FAZEU SZUTF KDQHQ

"Well, that's definitely not a pigpen cipher," Justin said. "But there is good news."

"There is?" I asked.

"Sure," he replied. "Two good things, actually. First, it looks like it is a cipher instead of a code. If it was a code, we'd probably be out of luck unless we could find the codebook hidden somewhere in that library."

"Well, don't look at me to sneak back in there," Stephanie said. "I was scared to death."

"What's the other good news, Justin?" I asked.

Justin grinned. "Well, if it wasn't something important, someone wouldn't have gone to so much trouble to put it into a cipher."

He was probably right. Someone wanted to keep the information hidden, or at least hidden from anyone who couldn't figure it out.

"It doesn't make any sense though," said Stephanie. "It looks like all of the words are five letters long. That can't be right."

"It isn't," Justin said. "That's one way to make a

cipher more difficult to figure out. Here, let me show you."

He took another sheet of paper and wrote a single line of letters.

IREAL LYLIK ETODR INKLE MONAD EONAH OTSUM MERDAY

We looked at the letters but couldn't make any sense of them. "Is that in code?" Catherine asked.

"Nope, plain English," Justin said with a smile. "I just put all of the letters into blocks of five."

Knowing that, the sentence became easy to read. "I really like to drink lemonade on a hot summer day," Stephanie said.

"Exactly," Justin said. "We're used to reading words with upper and lower-case letters, punctuation, and spaces separating the words. When we put the same letters in all capitals and mess with the spacing, it's like we're reading a foreign language."

We looked back at the sheet of paper with the image Stephanie had taken from beneath one of the library chairs. Could it be as simple as just putting in the right spacing? We quickly found out that it wasn't. There was no way to make works out of the jumble of letters on the sheet.

"Okay, that tells us we're looking at some kind of cipher," I said thoughtfully.

"But how can we solve it?" asked Stephanie.

"Simple," Justin grinned. "We use math."

The three of us looked up in surprise. How could we use math to decipher a hidden message?

"I think it's a simple substitution cipher," he said.

"What do you mean?" I asked.

"A simple substitution cipher just means you replace one letter with another throughout the whole message," he explained. "And if it's a Caesar cipher, it will make our job that much easier."

"Caesar, like the Roman emperor?" Stephanie asked.

"Or Caesar, like the salad?" I quipped, drawing groans from my friends.

"Yes, it was named after Julius Caesar," Justin answered. "In a Caesar cipher, all of the letters are just shifted over some number of spaces. Here, let me show you."

Justin drew a quick diagram on a sheet of notebook paper.

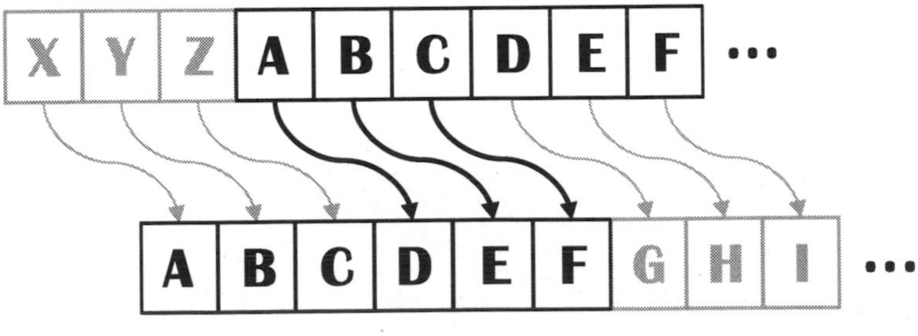

"The top boxes," he explained, "are the letters of the alphabet before we encrypt them. The bottom boxes are the encrypted alphabet. We just shift every letter over by three spaces."

"I get it," said Stephanie. "If I want to encrypt the letter *A*, I would put a *D* in my secret message."

"Right," Justin nodded. "And to decrypt, all we have to do is take the encrypted message and shift the same number of spaces in the opposite direction. I would shift the letter *D* three places to the left and I would get back to *A*."

"That's cool," said Catherine, "but how does math figure into it?"

"It's called letter frequency," Justin said. When we looked confused, he asked "You've all played the game Hangman, right?"

We nodded. We had all played Hangman, where you try to guess a word by choosing one letter at a time. If the letter was in the word, it was revealed in the word. If not, another part of a man was drawn. If the guesser could figure out the word before the man was "hanged," they won the game. If not, the guesser lost.

"When you play Hangman, what letter do you usually pick first?"

We all answered "*E*" in a single voice.

"Why?"

"Because there are more words with *E* in them," Catherine answered.

"Exactly," Justin said. "You wouldn't start with a letter like *Q* or *Z* or *X* or *J* because they don't show up in nearly as many words as *E*. The top letters used in the English language are *E*, *T*, *A*, *O*, *I*, and *N*."

Now it was starting to make sense. If the same letter was substituted throughout the cipher, we would see that some letters appeared much more frequently. Maybe one of those was an *E* or one of the other frequently used letters. That might be enough to get us started on solving the cipher!

We started by listing all the letters and counting how many times each was used in the cipher. Stephanie wrote out the list in her neat handwriting. Justin suggested we add a column that showed the frequency of each letter to make it easier to compare the incidences of letters in the message to the normal frequency we would expect to see.

It was easy to pick out the top letters. *Q* had the most with forty-two. Next came *E* and *F* with twenty-three each. Then came *A* and *U*, which each appeared twenty times in the cipher.

"Hey, can I use your computer for a minute?" Justin asked Stephanie.

Letter	Count	Frequency (%)
A	29	6.5
B	6	1.3
C	0	0.0
D	28	6.3
E	27	6.1
F	38	8.5
G	17	3.8
H	5	1.1
I	14	3.1
J	0	0.0
K	14	3.1
L	0	0.0
M	29	6.5
N	8	1.8
O	7	1.6
P	19	4.3
Q	65	14.8
R	12	2.7
S	7	1.6
T	27	6.1
U	30	6.8
V	1	0.2
W	4	0.9
X	20	4.5
Y	10	2.3
Z	23	5.2

"Sure," Stephanie replied. "What for?"

"I want to see if I can find the whole list of frequencies for each letter."

It only took a couple of minutes to find what he was looking for on the internet. Once he found it, Stephanie added the normal frequency to her list of letters.

Letter	Count	Frequency (%)	Normal (%)
A	29	6.5	8.2
B	6	1.3	1.5
C	0	0.0	2.8
D	28	6.3	4.3
E	27	6.1	12.7
F	38	8.5	2.2
G	17	3.8	2.0
H	5	1.1	6.1
I	14	3.1	7.0
J	0	0.0	0.2
K	14	3.1	0.8
L	0	0.0	4.0
M	29	6.5	2.4
N	8	1.8	6.7
O	7	1.6	7.5
P	19	4.3	1.9
Q	65	14.8	0.1
R	12	2.7	6.0
S	7	1.6	6.3
T	27	6.1	9.1
U	30	6.8	2.8
V	1	0.2	1.0
W	4	0.9	2.4
X	20	4.5	0.2
Y	10	2.3	2.0
Z	23	5.2	0.1

We stared at the columns of letters and numbers, trying to figure out where to start. Even Justin, who seemed to know a lot about ciphers, looked stumped. "Of course, if it's not a simple substitution cipher we'll probably never solve it," he said.

"What do you mean?" I asked.

"Well, sometimes the same letter in the cipher doesn't mean the same for the whole message. So, the letter *A* in one part of the cipher might stand for *M* but a different *A* might stand for the letter *B*."

"Like the Enigma machine!" Catherine exclaimed. "I remember reading about that. The same letter could be encrypted as different letters in the same message."

She went on to explain how Enigma was a clever machine used by the Germans in World War II. It used mechanical rotors to encrypt each letter multiple times. Without knowing how each of the rotors was set, it was almost impossible to decipher the messages. That was, of course, until Alan Turing and his team created a machine to try out thousands of possible combinations until the correct one was found. Countless lives were saved by knowing where and when German submarines were going to strike.

"I don't think this cipher is that complicated," Justin said confidently.

"Why not?" Catherine asked.

"Because I think Cletus wanted someone to figure it out," he said.

"Cletus?" I asked.

"Like in Cletus Maynard?" Stephanie added.

"Exactly!" Justin said.

"But how do you know it was Cletus who left the clue?" I asked incredulously.

"It's simple," Justin grinned. "Because he was the one who checked out the book."

Want to learn more about the Enigma machine? Check out the appendix at the end of the book!

Chapter 8

Justin was right. If it really had been Cletus Maynard that had checked out the book, he must have been the one who left the clue!

"But why do you think he wanted someone to figure it out?" I asked as we walked to school the next morning.

"Why even leave a clue if you don't want someone to figure it out?"

I couldn't argue with that logic. If Cletus really didn't want someone to find the secret, he wouldn't have even written it down. Still, he had hidden the first clue in an obscure book on the history of Maynard in writing so small that you had to really squint to see it.

"I think he figured someone would find it eventually," Justin countered, adding, "and he started off with a really easy cipher."

"I guess that's true," I conceded.

"No doubt about it," Justin said confidently. "He wanted someone to find the clue under the chair."

"But why?" I asked. "What is it he wanted us to figure out?"

"That's the question, isn't it?"

We pondered that question as we walked.

"So, Cletus disappeared in 1965, right?" I said. "But then he's back in town again in 1984, if that's really the same Cletus who checked out the book. Where did he go? And why did he come back?"

More questions to think about. Unfortunately, it seemed that every question led to even more.

We had just entered the school yard when Justin stopped dead in his tracks. I walked on another ten feet before I realized he was no longer walking next to me. I turned and saw him staring off into the distance. I waited for him to finish thinking through whatever was going through his mind.

"What if Cletus didn't write that code back in 1984?" Justin asked.

"You think maybe it was someone else?"

There was no immediate response from my friend. I could tell he was still thinking it through. After another long period of silence, he spoke again.

"Why do you think he used two different codes?" he asked.

"What do you mean?"

"He used a pigpen cipher for the first code, but then went to a more sophisticated one for the second."

"Maybe he wanted to make the first one easier for someone to decode," I said.

"Maybe," Justin said thoughtfully. "Or maybe he did it because it was easier for him to encode it in the first place."

"What do you mean?"

"What if he had lots of time to come up with the second code, but only had a few minutes for the first?"

"Why didn't he have more time for the first code?" I asked.

"Maybe because he didn't write the code into the book in 1984."

"Then when did he do it?"

"What if he wrote it right under Stephanie's nose?"

The first bell rang, signaling only ten minutes before school started. Justin didn't add anything to his cryptic comment as we hustled into the building.

Chapter 9

Still a couple of blocks from school, Stephanie and Catherine were also discussing Cletus and the coded message.

"I think Justin is right," Catherine said.

"About Cletus leaving the clue?" Stephanie asked.

"Yes. It doesn't make sense for anyone else to have left it. And besides, who else besides Cletus could have left a clue under a chair in his own library?"

"One of the tour guides maybe?"

"Maybe, but Cletus was the last one to check out the book. Whoever wrote the code in the book had to be the same person who wrote the code under the chair."

Catherine's logic made sense, but that just raised more questions. What was it that Cletus wanted someone to know? And why now?

"Not to change the subject, but have you heard anything new on the budget cuts at school?" Stephanie asked. "My parents weren't able to make it to the meeting last night."

"My dad went to the meeting, but he told me nothing much has really changed. If they can't come up with some additional revenue for the town, the cuts will have to go through."

"That really stinks," Stephanie said sadly. "I was really looking forward to seeing if we could beat the other schools at the math competition."

"Yeah, me too," Catherine responded. "My dad said some of the parents were really mad last night. Brian Brown's dad threatened to take one of the town council members out behind the school."

"That sure sounds like Brian's dad, all right," Stephanie said with grin. "And you wonder where Brian gets it."

"The apple sure didn't fall far from that tree," Catherine agreed.

Brian and his friends were not exactly fans of the Math Kids. The club had had run-ins with them the entire year.

They walked on in silence for a few minutes. Suddenly Stephanie slowed to a stop. Catherine looked back at her.

"What if…" Stephanie said.

"What if what?"

"What if the clue leads to a treasure?" Stephanie asked excitedly.

Catherine looked at her skeptically.

"Wait. Hear me out. Cletus Maynard was rich, right? He lived in a mansion, didn't he?"

"So, what makes you think he left a treasure behind?" Catherine asked.

"Think about it. He's a rich guy with no kids or known relatives. All he has is his wife. Then she dies, and he just disappears. So, where did all of his money go?"

"How should I know?"

"Well, here's what I think. I think he put all his

money in a big old chest and then left clues for us to find it. I think there's a treasure out there just waiting for us!"

"That would be cool, Stephanie," Catherine said. "What would you do with the money if you found the treasure?"

"That's easy," Stephanie grinned. "I'd give it to the school so we could have our math competition. What do you think?"

"I think you might be overly optimistic." Catherine responded. "And you know what else I think?"

"What?"

"I think if we don't hurry, we're going to be late for school," Catherine said.

The girls smiled and picked up their pace.

Chapter 10

With the math competition canceled, Mrs. Gouche took it easy on us during the week. With no tough problems to solve, we used our math group time to try to solve the chair clue. Despite repeated attempts, we were no closer to solving the message when Friday rolled around.

"We need to come up with a better way to look at the problem," Catherine proclaimed.

"What do you mean?" I asked.

"We just keep staring at the paper," she replied. "We're not getting anywhere, and it's starting to give me a headache."

"What did you have in mind?" Stephanie asked.

"What if we graphed the letter frequencies? That might make something stand out," she said.

Catherine made a great point. If there was one thing I'd learned about math problems, it was that if one method of solving it wasn't working, it was time to try something different.

We got some graph paper from Mrs. Gouche and started to draw. We decided that a bar chart would be the best way to show the data. We put the letters across the bottom and the frequency along the left side. Thirty minutes later, we had a nice graph of the frequencies for the secret message. Below that we put the graph of the normal frequencies.

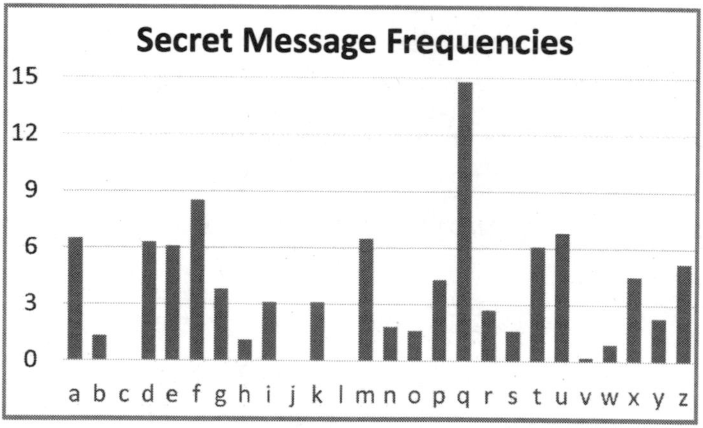

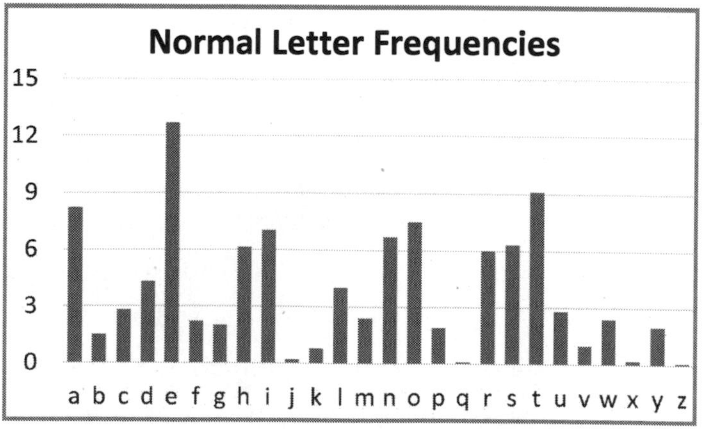

Catherine was the first to see it.

Catherine was right! Looking at the two graphs next to each, it became clear what Cletus had done.

"Look at E, F, G, H, and I on the lower graph, the normal letter frequencies," she said excitedly.

We all looked carefully at the five letters she had pointed out on the normal graph.

"Okay, so what?" I asked.

"Now look at *Q, R, S, T, U* on the frequency graph for the secret message," she said.

We looked, and now we saw what she was talking about. The graph for *E, F, G, H,* and *I* on the normal graph looked almost identical to the graph for *Q, R, S, T, U* on the coded graph.

"Then that means he just shifted the letters over!" Justin yelled. Mrs. Gouche looked up from the papers she was grading but didn't say anything. She was used to us getting excited about solving problems and yelling out in class, even though we weren't really supposed to do so.

"So maybe it's one of those salad ciphers," I said. "You know, Caesar."

"It wasn't funny the first time, dude," Justin said, getting nods of agreement from Stephanie and Catherine.

"Hey, I gave it a shot." I shrugged.

Justin grabbed a piece of paper and quickly began to write. He was writing so fast that his pencil was a blur. Unfortunately, so were the letters he was writing. His handwriting wasn't very good when he took his time, but when he was writing quickly it was an illegible mess.

"Um, maybe we should have Stephanie write down whatever it is you're trying to write," I suggested.

He looked down at the scribbled mess.

"Yeah, that's probably a good idea," he said sheepishly.

He explained to Stephanie what he was trying to write.

"The *Q* is really an *E*. The *R* is an *F*. The *S* is a *G*. Got it?"

Stephanie got it. She took a fresh sheet of paper and wrote down the key for deciphering the message.

"The top line is the coded letter," she explained, "and the bottom line is the decoded letter."

a	b	c	d	e	f	g	h	i	j	k	l	m	n	o	p	q	r	s	t	u	v	w	x	y	z
O	P	Q	R	S	T	U	V	W	X	Y	Z	A	B	C	D	E	F	G	H	I	J	K	L	M	N

Stephanie used our new letter map and started writing down the deciphered message. We crowded around her as she wrote, getting closer and closer until she finally had to ask us to give her a little space so she could work. We could feel the excitement building as she neared the end of the clue.

Was this it? Had we really solved the puzzle?

Stephanie finished writing. We looked down at the sheet of paper. Our hearts fell when we saw what she had written.

TIFOT	*HGUOH*	*TEHEM*	*ITYRE*	*VEHGU*	*ALREH*
TAFDN	*ARGYM*	*EDAMT*	*AHTEC*	*ALPAN*	*INEDD*
IHSIH	*TAPEU*	*RTEHT*	*NOITA*	*NITSE*	*DEHTH*
CAERU	*OYERO*	*FEBDE*	*KCOLB*	*EBLLI*	*WYENR*
UOJRU	*OYTUB*	*KEESU*	*OYREB*	*MUNEH*	*TSIEN*
IN-YTN	*EVESS*	*CITIL*	*OPWOL*	*LOFTO*	*NODOH*
WESOH	*TROFD*	*ENIAG*	*REHTA*	*FDNAR*	*GYMWO*
HSITS	*OLEHW*	*OHDEE*	*NDLUO*	*WUOYS*	*EULCE*
HTLLA	*EDIVO*	*RPDLU*	*OWERU*	*LIAFL*	*AITNE*
DISER	*PADEL*	*AEVER*	*TSRIF*	*SAWTI*	*HCIHW*
MORFS	*SENKR*	*ADEHT*	*YBDER*	*EVOCE*	*RTUBD*
NUOFS	*AWTIE*	*REHWS*	*NIAME*	*RERUS*	*AERTE*
HTTNE	*REFFI*	*DYLER*	*ITNEG*	*NIHTE*	*MOSSD*
LEIYK	*EESEW*	*TAHWS*	*EMITE*	*MOSSR*	*AEPPA*
TISAS	*YAWLA*	*TONSI*	*GNIHT*	*YREVE*	

It was gibberish. We hadn't solved the puzzle after all.

Chapter 11

"Why is it so cold in here?" Stephanie asked as she entered the classroom on Monday morning.

"They turned all the thermostats down to save money," Justin answered.

"I guess I'm keeping this thing on then," Stephanie said as she pulled her jacket a little closer. It had been an unseasonably cool spring and the misting rain outside made things seem even colder.

"These budget cuts stink," Catherine said. "First they canceled our math competition, and now they're trying to freeze us to death."

Everyone was in a somber mood. It had been three days since we thought we had decrypted the mysterious clue from under the chair in the old Maynard mansion library, only to find out we hadn't come close.

"It doesn't make any sense," Justin continued to complain. The letter frequency was almost a perfect match to the normal frequency."

Nothing irritated Justin more than not being able to solve a problem, especially when he thought he had come up with the perfect plan for doing it. And in this case, we all shared his frustration. If he was right about the letter frequency, then we should have been able to read the message.

"I bet we're missing something right in front of our eyes," he said as he stared down at Stephanie's neat handwriting. "Are you sure you got every letter translated correctly?"

Stephanie looked at him with irritation.

"I mean, are you sure you didn't shift it the wrong direction?"

"Feel free to check it yourself, Justin," she said snippily. "I went back and double- and triple-checked it. Every letter is translated just like you told me."

Justin looked carefully at the message, checking every letter. Stephanie was right. She had translated it perfectly.

"I'm sorry, Stephanie," he said quietly. "You got every letter right."

"Except the hyphen," I said.

"The what?" Justin asked.

"The hyphen," I answered. "She didn't include the hyphen."

"Wait a minute," Justin said. "What is a hyphen doing in there?"

That question ended up being the key to everything.

We looked closely at the blocks of letters around the hyphen.

TSIEN IN-YTN EVESS

It still looked like gibberish to me, but the look on Catherine's face said it all. She had it!

"It's a number!" she blurted out.

"What's a number?" I asked. "I mean, I know what a number is, but what are you talking about?"

"Seventy-nine!" Catherine said with a squeal of joy.

I looked again, and that's when I finally understood. It was backwards! The message was written backwards!

It only took Stephanie a couple of minutes to rewrite the message, this time starting with the last letter instead of the first. We broke into cheers as we all high-fived each other.

"That's enough!" Mrs. Gouche said sharply.

We quieted down, but there was no way to conceal our excitement as we read the decrypted message.

Everything is not always as it appears. Sometimes what we seek yields something entirely different. The treasure remains where it was found but recovered by the darkness from which it was first revealed. A presidential failure would provide all the clues you would need. How he lost is how my grandfather gained. For those who do not follow politics, seventy-nine is the number you seek, but your journey will be blocked before you reach the destination. The true path is hidden in a place that made my grandfather laugh every time he thought of it.

We had done it! The message was decrypted.

"I was right!" Stephanie said. "There is a treasure!"

That part of the message was clear. The rest, however, wasn't. What was Cletus trying to tell us? What was the treasure and where was it hidden? What did he mean when he said our journey would be blocked? And what did the sentence about his grandfather mean?

"Looks like we've got another puzzle to solve," Justin said, his eyes lighting up. The rest of us were excited too. Like Justin, the rest of us Math Kids loved a good puzzle!

Chapter 12

On Wednesday, we had a day off school because of teacher meetings. We used the free day to have an impromptu Math Kids meeting in my basement. It was a perfect time to make our first attempt at solving the puzzle.

We decided to break the clue down into parts:

1) The treasure remains where it was found
2) Presidential failure (how he lost provides clues)
3) 79 is the number you seek
4) Journey will be blocked
5) True path is hidden in a place that made Cletus's grandfather laugh

Unfortunately, that didn't give us much to go on. All the clues were very obscure, except for the number seventy-nine. That one was clear, but we still had no idea what it meant.

"Why would we seek the number seventy-nine?" Catherine asked.

"You got me," I answered. "It makes it sound like seventy-nine is the treasure, or it somehow leads to the treasure."

"And if our journey is going to be blocked, does that mean we can't find it even if we try?" Catherine asked.

"Oh, I think we can find it," Justin said confidently. "I think Cletus wants us to find it."

"But why?" I asked. "If it's a treasure, why didn't he just claim it for himself?"

That was one question we all agreed on—if there was really a treasure, why did Cletus want someone else to find it? And where had Cletus gone when he disappeared?

"Well, at least we know that the treasure has been hidden for some time, since it mentions that his grandfather gained from it," Stephanie said.

"Also, the true path is hidden in a place that made him laugh, whatever that means," I added.

"What are our next steps?" Justin asked.

That question told us that Justin was ready to get down to business. He always thinks things out in a very logical manner. He treats everything like he's solving a math problem, by going step by step. Unfortunately, there were no equations to solve here, no patterns to observe, no mathematical concepts that would help us along our way.

"I'm going back to the library," Stephanie announced.

"What for?" I asked.

"Cletus put the first coded message in a book for us to find, but it wasn't obvious. I'm going to find out what was on the page where he left the message and see if that provides a clue," she answered.

We all agreed that was a great idea.

"I'm going to check with my dad about the number seventy-nine," Catherine said.

Catherine knew that every number has something special about it. Some numbers, like her favorite, 55, had lots of special qualities. Most importantly, she knew that 55 was the tenth number in the Fibonacci series, and that knowledge had won the fourth-grade math contest for us and put us into the district-wide competition. Unfortunately, that contest wasn't going to happen now. But if anyone could find out what was special about a number, it was Catherine.

"How about you, Jordan?" Stephanie asked.

"Well, I guess it's time for me to learn a little more about presidential elections," I smiled. "I guess I'll be going to the library too."

"And that just leaves you, Justin. What's your plan?" Catherine asked.

"I'm headed home for a snack," he said with a grin.

We all looked at him in surprise. "There's also something there I want to check out," he added.

He didn't say anything more, but by now we were used to Justin keeping quiet about his plans, so we didn't even bother to ask.

We set off in three different directions. Stephanie and I headed for the library, Catherine for the college, and Justin for home. We were each on our own quest for information. Would it be enough to figure out the cryptic message?

Chapter 13

When Catherine arrived at the college, her dad was teaching a freshman Algebra class, so she wandered around the math and science building where he taught. She didn't mind the wait because it was one of her favorite places to be. She loved to peek into the computer science rooms at the students working on various projects, their heads down as they stared at their laptop screens and their fingers flew over the keyboards. She loved to look at the bulletin boards crowded with colored sheets of paper advertising tutoring, campus clubs, university events, and her favorite, math challenges. She knew she didn't know enough higher-level math to do any of the challenges right now, but it was exciting to think that one day she would be able to do them.

The door to her dad's classroom opened and students began to fill the hallway. Her father finally emerged, and Catherine gave him a wave. He returned the wave and then pointed at his watch and held up the fingers on both hands. Catherine got the message. He was going to be another ten minutes. He was probably headed to his office to help one of his students.

Catherine wandered toward the far end of the hallway where the professors' offices were, keeping to one side so as not to get run over by the parade of students. Some were talking animatedly to classmates while others were checking their phones for any messages they might have missed during class.

Catherine ducked into a doorway to let a crowd of students pass. When she looked around, she found herself in one of the chemistry rooms. She looked at the wall of equipment, which included beakers, test tubes, and rows of carefully labeled chemicals. But it was something else that caught her eye.

A giant chart hung on one wall. Catherine's dad had shown her this chart before. It was called the periodic table, and it listed all the chemical elements, like oxygen, carbon, and lead, all ordered by their atomic number.

She was staring at the chart when her father entered the room.

"Oh, there you are," he said. "I thought I might find you in here."

"Hi Dad," Catherine said, giving him a quick hug without taking her eyes from the chart.

"You aren't going to break my heart and study chemistry instead of math, are you?" he asked with a twinkle in his eye.

"No, but I love looking at the periodic table. What do the different rows and columns mean?"

"They help to classify the elements," Mr. Duchesne explained. "The column on the right contains the noble gases. The bottom row is the actinides, and the elements in the middle are called transition metals."

The Periodic Table Of The Elements

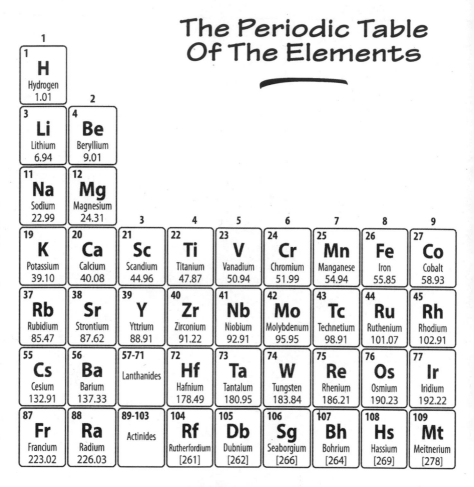

1	2	3	4	5	6	7	8	9
1 H Hydrogen 1.01								
3 Li Lithium 6.94	4 Be Beryllium 9.01							
11 Na Sodium 22.99	12 Mg Magnesium 24.31							
19 K Potassium 39.10	20 Ca Calcium 40.08	21 Sc Scandium 44.96	22 Ti Titanium 47.87	23 V Vanadium 50.94	24 Cr Chromium 51.99	25 Mn Manganese 54.94	26 Fe Iron 55.85	27 Co Cobalt 58.93
37 Rb Rubidium 85.47	38 Sr Strontium 87.62	39 Y Yttrium 88.91	40 Zr Zirconium 91.22	41 Nb Niobium 92.91	42 Mo Molybdenum 95.95	43 Tc Technetium 98.91	44 Ru Ruthenium 101.07	45 Rh Rhodium 102.91
55 Cs Cesium 132.91	56 Ba Barium 137.33	57-71 Lanthanides	72 Hf Hafnium 178.49	73 Ta Tantalum 180.95	74 W Tungsten 183.84	75 Re Rhenium 186.21	76 Os Osmium 190.23	77 Ir Iridium 192.22
87 Fr Francium 223.02	88 Ra Radium 226.03	89-103 Actinides	104 Rf Rutherfordium [261]	105 Db Dubnium [262]	106 Sg Seaborgium [266]	107 Bh Bohrium [264]	108 Hs Hassium [269]	109 Mt Meitnerium [278]

57 La Lanthanum 138.91	58 Ce Cerium 140.12	59 Pr Praseodymium 140.91	60 Nd Neodymium 144.24	61 Pm Promethium 144.91	62 Sm Samarium 150.36	63 Eu Europium 151.96
89 Ac Actinium 227.03	90 Th Thorium 232.04	91 Pa Protactinium 231.04	92 U Uranium 238.03	93 Np Neptunium 237.05	94 Pu Plutonium 244.06	95 Am Americium 243.06

An Encrypted Clue

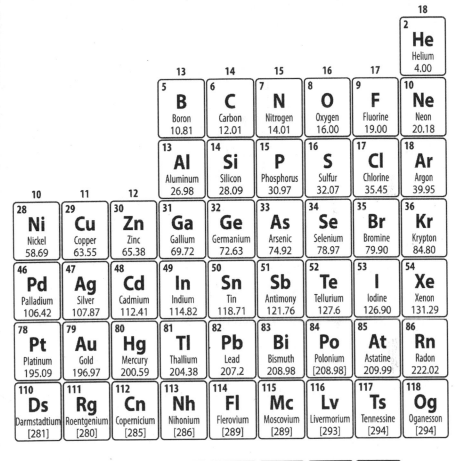

10	11	12	13	14	15	16	17	18
								2 **He** Helium 4.00
			5 **B** Boron 10.81	6 **C** Carbon 12.01	7 **N** Nitrogen 14.01	8 **O** Oxygen 16.00	9 **F** Fluorine 19.00	10 **Ne** Neon 20.18
			13 **Al** Aluminum 26.98	14 **Si** Silicon 28.09	15 **P** Phosphorus 30.97	16 **S** Sulfur 32.07	17 **Cl** Chlorine 35.45	18 **Ar** Argon 39.95
28 **Ni** Nickel 58.69	29 **Cu** Copper 63.55	30 **Zn** Zinc 65.38	31 **Ga** Gallium 69.72	32 **Ge** Germanium 72.63	33 **As** Arsenic 74.92	34 **Se** Selenium 78.97	35 **Br** Bromine 79.90	36 **Kr** Krypton 84.80
46 **Pd** Palladium 106.42	47 **Ag** Silver 107.87	48 **Cd** Cadmium 112.41	49 **In** Indium 114.82	50 **Sn** Tin 118.71	51 **Sb** Antimony 121.76	52 **Te** Tellurium 127.6	53 **I** Iodine 126.90	54 **Xe** Xenon 131.29
78 **Pt** Platinum 195.09	79 **Au** Gold 196.97	80 **Hg** Mercury 200.59	81 **Tl** Thallium 204.38	82 **Pb** Lead 207.2	83 **Bi** Bismuth 208.98	84 **Po** Polonium [208.98]	85 **At** Astatine 209.99	86 **Rn** Radon 222.02
110 **Ds** Darmstadtium [281]	111 **Rg** Roentgenium [280]	112 **Cn** Copernicium [285]	113 **Nh** Nihonium [286]	114 **Fl** Flerovium [289]	115 **Mc** Moscovium [289]	116 **Lv** Livermorium [293]	117 **Ts** Tennessine [294]	118 **Og** Oganesson [294]

64 **Gd** Gadolinium 157.25	65 **Tb** Terbium 158.93	66 **Dy** Dysprosium 162.50	67 **Ho** Holmium 164.93	68 **Er** Erbium 167.26	69 **Tm** Thulium 168.93	70 **Yb** Ytterbium 173.06	71 **Lu** Lutetium 174.97
96 **Cm** Curium 247.07	97 **Bk** Berkelium 247.07	98 **Cf** Californium 251.08	99 **Es** Einsteinium [254]	100 **Fm** Fermium 257.10	101 **Md** Mendelevium 258.1	102 **No** Nobelium 259.10	103 **Lr** Lawrencium [262]

Her dad went on, but Catherine was no longer listening because there it was, near the right side of the transition metals.

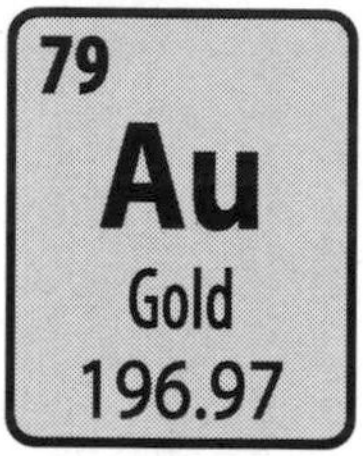

She stepped closer, and a broad smile came across her face. *Seventy-nine is the number you seek*, the clue read. The number seventy-nine was the number for gold on the periodic table! Was that it? Was the treasure gold?

"Thanks, dad. I gotta run," she said, already headed for the door to the hallway.

Her father called out to her. "You came all this way and you're already leaving?" he asked.

"Yeah, sorry Dad, but I just thought of something. I need to go to the library," she answered.

He looked like he was going to say something more, but she turned and headed off before he could ask any more questions.

"Kids," she heard him mutter as she was leaving the room. "Was I like that when I was her age?"

Chapter 14

"Justin, how many times have I told you not to eat cookies on the couch?" his mother asked.

"I'm going to guess about a million," he answered, smiling broadly. He had found that he could get away with a little sass with his mom as long as he followed it up with a big smile.

His mom shook her head, trying not to smile at her son's reply.

Justin popped the last cookie into his mouth and went back to the book he was poring over. He was in the middle of *The Caves of Northern Virginia*, reading a chapter on cave disasters.

In particular, he was reading about cave-in in 1908 that had caused a landslide and trapped eleven coal miners underground just outside of Maynard. There had been almost eight straight days of rain, and water had filled a large pool sitting over the primary tunnel used by the Maynard Mining Company. The pressure from the weight of the water had grown until it finally collapsed the tunnel roof. The water and debris cascaded into the tunnel, tearing out a large section of the cave wall and trapping the miners behind a wall of stone.

Because the tunnel was now filled with water, it was impossible to get to the trapped miners through the main entrance. So, desperate to get to them, another team of miners led by Eustis Maynard immediately began working on a second tunnel into the cave. It was slow work because they needed to bore through almost a hundred yards of rock to get around to the other side of the landslide. Even working around the clock, it still took almost six days for the rescuers to reach the miners, and by the time the rescuers arrived, all eleven trapped miners had died.

Justin and his friends had ridden their bikes up to the cave entrance before. A tall, sturdy chain link fence prevented them from getting any closer than fifty feet to the entrance. Rusted signs warned of the danger in going into the cave, but there wasn't a way to get in even if they had ignored the signs and scaled the twelve-foot fence. The cave entrance itself was blocked with a securely padlocked iron gate. The gate was covered in dirt and rust, but it still looked plenty capable of keeping people out.

Justin looked down at the decrypted message and underlined several passages.

Everything is not always as it appears. Sometimes what we seek yields something entirely different. The treasure remains where it was found but recovered by the darkness from which it was first revealed. A presidential failure would be all the clues you would need. How he lost is how my grandfather gained. For those who do not follow politics, seventy-nine is the number you seek, but your journey will be blocked before you reach the destination. The true path is hidden in a place that made my grandfather laugh every time he thought of it.

If Cletus Maynard was the one who left the message, he would probably know all about the cave system. It was the basis for the Maynard family fortune, after all. Was this what Cletus was trying to tell them? Was the treasure, whatever it was, hidden in the caves?

At first, the thought excited Justin. He may not know what the treasure was, but he thought he at least a good idea of *where* it was. His excitement was quickly quashed when he realized the message was right—if the treasure was really in the cave, their journey was blocked before they even got started.

But then he remembered the last line of the message:

The true path is hidden in a place that made my grandfather laugh every time he thought of it.

That had to mean there was another way to get to the treasure!

He gathered up the book and the notes he had written, shoving everything into his already stuffed backpack. He was halfway out the door when his mother called out to him.

"Where are you headed, Justin?" she asked.

"To the library," he called back.

"Don't let the door—" she started to say, but it was too late. Justin let the door slam shut behind him and walked quickly away.

Chapter 15

Stephanie and I split up when we got to the library. She went to find *A Short History of Maynard*, the book that had started everything. She wanted to know what else was on page 213 besides the pigpen cipher that we now thought had been written by Cletus Maynard.

I was on my own search. I wanted to see what I could find out about presidential failures. After all, the message said that a presidential failure would provide all the clues we would need. I looked down at the message again.

A presidential failure would provide all the clues you would need. How he lost is how my grandfather gained.

What had he lost? A war? That could be considered a failure, right? What else can a president lose? I looked down at the message again and paused. The message didn't say *what* he lost but *how* he lost. What did that mean?

Our class had studied the presidents in third

grade. We each had to pick a president and do a presentation to the class. Everyone wanted to do one of the more famous presidents like Washington or Lincoln, so by the time I got to choose, all the good ones had already been taken. I ended up with Gerald Ford. He became vice president when Spiro Agnew resigned and then became president when Richard Nixon resigned. That made him the only president who wasn't elected to either president or vice president. A year after my presentation, that was pretty much all I could remember about President Ford.

Was it Richard Nixon? He lost the presidency when he resigned. I guess you could call that a big presidential failure. I thought about that for a minute but couldn't figure out how that could provide the clues we would need. Another thought occurred to me. If Cletus Maynard had left the clue on the bottom of the chair in the library, then he had left the house in 1965, so the message had to be referring to a president from before then.

I looked at who was president in 1965 when Cletus had disappeared. Lyndon B. Johnson. Had he had a big loss? I listed out facts about Johnson, hoping to find anything that looked like a clue.

Became president after John F. Kennedy was assassinated

Passed the Civil Rights Act in 1964
Beat Barry Goldwater in a landslide in the 1964 election
Passed the Voting Rights Act in 1965

Wait a minute—did I just miss something important?

Maybe it wasn't Johnson I should be looking at, but someone else entirely. I looked back at the third fact I had written.

Beat Barry Goldwater in a landslide in the 1964 election

Barry Goldwater had lost in a landslide! In fact, it was the worst defeat in the history of presidential elections when Johnson got more than 61 percent of the vote. Was that the presidential failure Cletus was talking about in his message?

A presidential failure would provide all the clues you would need. How he lost is how my grandfather gained.

But how did Cletus's grandfather gain from a landslide?

My thoughts on that were interrupted when Stephanie came running over to my table. She had *A Short History of Maynard* open to page 213. When she placed the book on the table, I could just make out the tiny writing in the right-hand column, the pigpen cipher that had first drawn her attention.

But it was the title at the top of the page that caught my attention:

Horrific Landslide Traps Miners

Ten minutes later, we had been joined by Justin and Catherine, and that's when we put all the pieces together.

It's funny, sometimes, how things can come together. We set out in four different directions, each ready to research our own topic. None of what we learned by ourselves would have been enough, but together, as a team, we learned everything we needed to know.

Catherine told us of her discovery in the college chemistry lab. Was Cletus telling us that the treasure was gold?

Stephanie showed the heading of the chapter where she had found the pigpen cipher. The clue was pointing to the landslide having something to do with the treasure.

Justin provided more information on the landslide from what he had found in *The Caves of Northern Virginia*.

And this time, it was me who put it all together.

"Cletus was right," I said. "The 1964 election results really did give us all the clues we needed."

I wrote it down on a piece of paper so they could see it for themselves.

Barry Goldwater lost in a landslide

"Don't you get it?" I asked.

Seeing their puzzled faces, I spelled it out for them.

Buried gold lost in a landslide

"But if the gold is lost, how does that help us?" Stephanie asked.

"I don't think the gold is lost," Justin replied. "In fact, I think the landslide helped the gold to be found in the first place. Remember what the message said? *Sometimes what we seek yields something entirely different.* When the landslide happened, the cave wall was ripped apart. They had been seeking coal, but maybe what Cletus's grandfather found behind that wall was gold!"

"It also says our journey will be blocked," Catherine said.

"Well, if it's in that cave, it's definitely blocked," I said. "There's a big fence and a locked gate at the entrance."

"I've got an idea on that too," Justin said. "The message says there is another path, the true path. It's hidden in a place that always made Cletus's grandfather laugh."

"So, you're saying there is another way into the cave without going through the main tunnel?" I asked.

"That's right," Justin said confidently. "We'll just go in the way they did when they found the gold—the same path they used to get to the trapped miners in the first place."

Chapter 16

Justin explained what he had learned about the long-ago attempted rescue of the miners trapped in the landslide. He spread a map of the cave system on the table. It was a geologic map showing elevations and all the landforms in the area.

"Here's the cave entrance," he said, pointing to a spot he had marked with a large red *X*. "The cave-in was sixty feet from the entrance. That would be right about here." He made a smaller *X* at that spot.

"The book said they tunneled through three hundred feet of rock to reach them," he said. "That means they could have started anywhere on this circle." He used a compass to make a dashed circle measuring three hundred feet from the location of the cave-in.

"Notice anything?" he asked.

We looked carefully at the map and the circle he had drawn. The circle went right through a large rectangular shape to the north of the cave entrance.

"What's this shape here?" I asked.

Justin smiled. "That just so happens to be the Maynard House."

"Are you telling us you think the rescue tunnel goes all the way to the house?" Stephanie asked.

"Not just to the house," Justin replied. "I think it goes all the way into the basement in the new section of the mansion."

"You think they used the excavated land as part of the basement when Eustis added the east wing?" I asked.

"I guess that would have saved him some money because the hole was already there," Catherine said.

"I don't think it was to save him money," Justin said. "He and his brother were already the richest men in town."

"Then why did he do it?" Catherine asked.

"I think he did it to hide the entrance to the tunnel," Justin answered. "Think about it. If he found gold in the tunnel, he wanted to make sure no one else could get to it."

"Except us, that is!" I said.

"So how do we get to it?" Stephanie asked.

"We need to get into the basement of the house," Justin said. "If I'm right about the final clue, I think I know just where to find the tunnel."

For the next hour, we discussed Justin's plan for

getting us into the basement and, if we were right, all the way to the golden treasure. We decided that Saturday was our best chance because the crowds visiting the mansion would be larger and it would be easier to slip away from the group and into the basement.

We were still deep in conversation as we left the library. As we reached the sidewalk, I looked back toward the building and caught a glimpse of the man with the beard, the same man we saw on the way to the mansion. He was looking at us through the window. When he saw me looking back at him, he turned away quickly. I started to say something but found I'd fallen behind and had to run to catch up with my friends.

The rest of the week went by as slowly as the last week of school. We met every day to plan our trip back to the Maynard mansion. Our idea was slowly coming together. We just needed a little luck.

Saturday finally came, and Catherine's dad drove us up the long winding hill to the mansion. It was a beautiful sunny day and the temperature was warmer than it had been all week.

"Seems to me like it's too nice a day to be inside some stuffy old house," Mr. Duchesne said as he reached the circular drive.

"It's for a school project, Dad," Catherine said as he pulled to a stop in front of the house.

"Okay, I'll pick you up in three hours," he said.

"Make it four," I chimed in quickly. "We might want to take the tour a couple of times."

"Must be some project," Mr. Duchesne said with a raised eyebrow.

We hopped out of the car before he could say anything more. As he drove off, we looked around the parking area and were happy to see several dozen cars already parked. We were hoping for a big crowd so we wouldn't be noticed as we slipped away from the others.

We had decided to split up into two groups to be less noticeable. Justin and I would go in first, and Stephanie and Catherine would join the next group. We paid at the front entrance and waited for our group to be called.

When it was time for our tour group, I looked at Justin. "Are you ready for this?"

Justin adjusted his backpack, which was, as always, bursting at the seams. I couldn't wait to see what he had brought with him this time. "Let's do it," he answered. His face looked confident, but he sounded nervous. I looked up at the imposing house, my eye drawn to the middle window where I had seen the light on that rainy night.

Chapter 17

Stephanie and Catherine walked over to one of the benches lining the circular drive.

"This cipher stuff is really interesting," Stephanie said. "I'm reading a book on Elizabeth Smith."

"Who's that?"

"She was one of the codebreakers in World War I. She and a guy named William Friedman were two of the first people to use letter frequency to crack codes."

"That's cool," Catherine said.

"It gets even cooler. After the war she joined the Coast Guard and set up the first cryptoanalysis section. She helped to break encrypted messages sent by criminals who were trying to sell liquor during prohibition."

"Wow, she had her own section?" Catherine was completely captivated by the story now and leaned closer.

"Well, it was just her and an assistant, but they decoded thousands of messages and sent lots of people to jail, including some of Al Capone's gang!"

"Girls rock!" Catherine pumped her fist.

"And that's not all. In World War II she helped to smash a Nazi spy network that was trying to start revolutions down in South America."

"Wait, how come I've never heard of her?" Catherine asked.

"A lot of it was classified for a long time, so it's just now coming out."

"Can I borrow that book when you're done with it?" Catherine asked.

Stephanie didn't answer, she was staring at the other bench.

"Hey, does that guy look familiar?" Stephanie asked.

"What guy?" Catherine asked.

Stephanie nodded her head toward the bench to their left, where an old man in a worn overcoat sat by himself. Catherine took a long look and then nodded.

"I think I've seen him at the library the last couple of times we were there," she said.

"He also looks like the guy in front of my house earlier this week," Stephanie said under her breath.

"He was at your house?" Catherine asked in alarm.

"Yeah, last Friday when we were all at the library," she answered. "I had a funny feeling that someone was following me, but the only person I saw was way up the block from my house, so I didn't think anything more about it. When I looked out of my bedroom window a little while later though, there was this old guy standing in front of the house. When he saw me looking, he just turned and walked away."

"Did you tell your parents?"

"No, I figured it was just someone who was a little lost," Stephanie said. "But now I'm not so sure. It looks like that might be the same guy."

Catherine stole another glance at the old man. He looked harmless enough half dozing on a bench on this bright, sunny day, but maybe looks were deceiving. Had he been following them?

She turned back to Stephanie, whose face suddenly twisted in fear.

"He's coming this way!" she whispered.

Catherine turned back, and sure enough, the old man was shuffling toward them!

Chapter 18

Justin and I joined the back of a large group of people in the enormous entranceway to the mansion. This time Justin had promised to keep quiet and not draw any attention to himself. He adjusted his oversized backpack to fit more comfortably on his shoulders as our tour leader began his introduction. We were both glad to see it was a different guy than the one who had led our last tour two weeks earlier.

"Remember, if the guide says there were two thousand books donated, just go with it, okay?" I said.

"But it was really just one thousand two hundred and fifty," Justin protested.

At my stern look, he shrugged his shoulders. "Two thousand books it is," he said.

"Welcome to the Maynard House," the tour guide began. "The house was built in 1903 by Herbert Maynard. He was the founder and first mayor of Maynard, so he holds an important place in the history of our town."

"I'm just glad they called the town Maynard instead of Herbert," a man in the front row called out, drawing laughter from the crowd.

The tour guide went on with his introduction, but Justin and I weren't paying any attention to him. We were focused on how we were going to slip away from the rest of the crowd and get through the door to the basement.

Following the same route we had taken just a few weeks earlier, the guide led us through the dining room, the butler's pantry, and the kitchen.

"That should be the door to the basement," Justin whispered in my ear, nodding toward a door in the back wall of the kitchen.

After the kitchen, we went through several bedrooms, the music room, and the enormous ballroom. We looked through the doorway leading to the library, again blocked by the velvet rope. We tensed because it was almost time for us to make our move. After the library, we would make our way down the long hallway to the formal living room covered in beautiful tapestries and artwork. That would be the end of the tour and we would be escorted out the front door. This was our last opportunity to slip away from the crowd and make our way back to the basement door before the next tour came through.

The crowd made its way down the large hallway,

admiring the ornate framed paintings lining the walls. The tour guide was now at the far end of the hall, pointing out a large oil painting to an elderly couple and their grandchildren. The kids looked like they couldn't wait for the tour to be over.

It was now or never. We waited until the guide made the turn into the living room and then made our move. We ducked into a side hallway and ran as quickly and quietly as we could toward the kitchen, then we paused to see if our absence was noted. Luckily, it sounded like the crowd had moved on into the living room. We darted through the kitchen and to the door to the basement. Justin got there first and turned the handle on the door. We just had to slip through the door, and we were home free.

But the door was locked!

We didn't have much time. The next tour group would be coming through the kitchen in just a couple of minutes. We looked around the hallway, hoping to find a key hanging on a hook, but the walls were bare. We could just make out the next tour guide starting into his speech. "Welcome to the Maynard House," he said, the faint sound of his words echoing off the polished wooden floors and into the kitchen.

"What do we do?" I asked in a panicked voice.

"We've got to hide," Justin replied, frantically

looking around the kitchen. He pulled open a couple of cabinet doors, hoping to find a spot big enough for us to crawl into.

The voice from the foyer grew louder. The crowd was heading into the dining room. From there, the kitchen would be the next stop.

"The butler's pantry!" I whispered loudly.

We ducked into the large room off the kitchen, but we knew that wasn't going to work for long because the pantry was part of the tour. I was able to squeeze behind an enormous refrigerator, but that didn't leave a place for Justin.

"And this is the kitchen," the guide said. There were oohs and aahs from the crowd as they saw the size of the kitchen. "The Maynards loved to entertain, and this kitchen allowed a large team of chefs to cook for as many as a hundred people."

Next would be the butler's pantry. As soon as the guide opened the door, Justin would be in plain sight. We had run out of time. I could hear the handle on the door start to turn when a question from the crowd bought us a few precious seconds.

"How many cooks did the Maynards have?"

"Great question," the tour guide said. "When they were having a large dinner party..."

I didn't hear the rest because my heart was pounding

with fear. I took a quick peek around the refrigerator and saw the door start to open. I ducked back behind the refrigerator.

"This is the butler's pantry," the guide said. "The shelves and refrigerator could hold enough food to feed the family and guests for more than a month."

I could hear people moving around the pantry, but no one walked to the back. If they had, they would have seen me crouched behind the refrigerator. After a long, anxious minute, the pantry door closed, and I could hear the crowd leaving the kitchen.

No one had seen me in my hiding place, but how had they not seen Justin in plain sight? Emerging from behind the refrigerator, I glanced around, but Justin was nowhere to be found.

I was thinking that he had found some way to join in with the crowd when I heard my name in a loud whisper. The sound came again. It appeared to be coming right through the back wall of the pantry. As I looked on in amazement, an opening appeared in the wall as a small door slid open and Justin poked his head out. He was grinning from ear to ear.

"It's a dumbwaiter," he said.

"A what?" I asked.

He explained that a dumbwaiter was a small elevator used for moving objects instead of people. They used to be common for moving food from one floor to another, so they usually went through the kitchen. This one was a cube about four feet on each side.

"Jump in," he said. That was easy for Justin to say. He was the smallest kid in our class, so he fit into the space quite easily. It looked like a much tighter squeeze for me with him already in it. I was debating whether I wanted to get in when I heard a sound from the kitchen. Without a further thought, I scrambled into the dumbwaiter, squeezing in beside Justin and his oversized backpack. He reached a hand out and pushed the button marked *B*. He slid the door shut, plunging us into darkness.

The dumb waiter jerked its way down, finally settling to a stop with a bump. Justin cautiously lifted the door and we crawled out into the utter darkness of the basement. Justin pulled the door shut and there was a loud hum as the dumbwaiter automatically returned to the kitchen. Then there was absolute silence, the rock walls absorbing every sound except our hushed breathing.

"It's about time you guys got here," came a voice out of the darkness. I tried to scream, but I was so scared the only thing that came out of my mouth was a tiny squeak.

Justin fumbled in his backpack for a flashlight.

The strong beam of light played over Stephanie and Catherine standing against the rough concrete wall. They were shaking with laughter.

"What?"

"But, how did you...?"

"We took a shortcut," Catherine said with a smile.

Chapter 19

"Seriously, how did you get into the basement?" I asked. "The door was locked."

"It was the old man," Stephanie said.

"What old man?" Justin asked.

"The old man from the library," Stephanie answered.

Justin looked puzzled.

"The one with the beard?" I asked.

"Yeah," Stephanie said. "I saw him in the library the day I found the cipher in the book."

"I saw an old guy with a beard looking at us when we figured out the clue the other day," I said.

Stephanie nodded vigorously, her ponytail bouncing. "That's the one. He was outside the mansion while we were waiting for our tour."

Justin frowned. "This is getting creepy."

"I think he's been following us. Stephanie said she saw him outside her house too," Catherine added. "He started walking toward us, so we took off running. We ran around the house to get away from him."

I interrupted, "But that doesn't explain how—"

"He was still following us, so we looked for a door we could duck into," Stephanie continued. "That's when Catherine found the old coal chute. It's how they used to get coal for the furnace into the house for heating."

Catherine held her blackened hands in front of the flashlight beam. "It's a little dirty, but it works great!"

"Okay, now we just need to find the tunnel," I said.

Justin reached into his backpack and pulled out flashlights for each of us. For the next half hour, we carefully examined the interior of the basement, looking for some indication of a hidden door that would lead to the tunnel, but every wall appeared to be solid concrete.

"There must be a trap door in the floor," Catherine concluded, but that search proved fruitless as well. We were out of places to look.

"Um, guys," Stephanie said quietly as she tugged on her ponytail, "we've got a problem. We may be trapped in here. There's no way to climb out of the coal chute and you said the door to the basement is locked."

"And there aren't any windows," Catherine added nervously.

"But there must be some way to get to the tunnel

from here," I said. "Either that or we were wrong about the clues."

"The clues!" Justin said in excitement.

"What about them?" I asked.

"Remember the last line in the clue? The true path is hidden in a place that made Cletus's grandfather laugh every time he thought of it."

"So?"

"I think the entrance to the tunnel is through the coal bin!" Justin shouted, prompting the three of us to quickly shush him.

"That makes sense," said Catherine in agreement. "The Maynard family had made its money mining coal, and the route to the treasure was through the coal. I can see how that would have made him laugh."

"Then what are we waiting for?" Justin said. "To the tunnel!"

He reached into his backpack and started removing items. There were bandanas to put over our mouths to keep out the dust. There was a can of bright yellow spray paint.

"It's for marking our way in the tunnel," Justin explained.

The final item he removed from the backpack was a large ball of yarn.

"What's the string for?" I asked.

"It's a backup plan for the spray paint," Justin

explained. "We'll tie it to something in the basement and unroll it as we go. That way, we'll be sure we'll be able to find our way back."

I nodded as he explained. As always, Justin seemed to think of everything when he made a plan.

Once we knew where to look, finding the tunnel turned out to be easy. At the back of the coal bin was a cleverly concealed door that swung inward. Justin tied one end of the string to a pipe and we started down the tunnel. The walls were rough and there were thick timbers spaced every fifteen feet or so to help prevent cave-ins. Knowing the history of the cave, the rotting wood did little to reassure us that we wouldn't suffer the same fate as the doomed miners.

There were a few turns and several times we came to forks in the tunnel.

"Why didn't they just keep going straight?" I asked.

"They were probably trying to take advantage of any existing crevices in the stone to get to the miners quicker," Catherine surmised.

Several times we had to turn back and search the other fork. Once, we came across a large hole. I shined my light down and saw it dropped at least fifteen feet. If we had not been watching carefully and fallen down the hole, we would have been seriously hurt… or worse.

Justin sprayed a large *X* on the wall every thirty feet and whenever we came to a fork. Catherine carefully unrolled the string to mark our path. After walking for a couple of minutes, I pointed my light back toward the direction of the house, but the flashlight beam only showed the rough tunnel behind us.

Everyone was on edge, so when Justin stopped so suddenly that Stephanie bumped into him, we all yelped.

"Why'd you stop?" I asked in a loud whisper.

"Look," he answered.

As we looked past him, we could see why he'd stopped. We had reached the cave-in. The tunnel had widened, and it was clear we had reached the original cave area. The walls were farther apart and the ceiling much higher. A large tumble of boulders completely blocked the original tunnel, and a pool of stagnant water had formed where the cave floor slanted toward one wall.

As we shined our lights around the space, we were suddenly transported more than a hundred years into the past. A pickaxe leaned against one wall, as if just put down by a miner to take a rest from the backbreaking work of chipping coal out of the wall. A lantern still hung from one of the wooden timbers. A metal bucket stood in one corner. I looked in the bucket. It was dry, but a wooden dipper still stood at the ready for a miner to take a drink to wash coal dust from his mouth.

"It must have been horrible," said Stephanie in a quiet voice. "Trapped in here knowing there was probably no way you were ever going to get out alive."

We were quiet as we thought about that for a long moment. Finally, Justin broke the silence.

"Um, guys, there's another problem." Everyone looked at him expectantly. "I don't see anything that looks like treasure."

"Justin's right," Jordan said. "Everybody spread out and see if you see anything."

We played our lights carefully around the space. Besides the few items left behind, we saw nothing but walls of blackness.

It looked like all we had done was for nothing. There was no treasure.

"This can't be right," said Justin. "The treasure has to be here somewhere."

"Maybe someone has already taken it," I frowned.

"Wait a minute," Catherine said. "Read the clue again."

Justin pulled a sheet of paper from his backpack. In the beam of his flashlight, he read the clue.

"Everything is not always as it appears. Sometimes what we seek yields something entirely different. The treasure remains where it was found but recovered by the darkness from which it was first revealed," he read before he was interrupted by a shriek from Catherine.

"That's it!" she yelled.

"What's it?" I asked.

"That's the clue we needed. Don't you see?" Catherine said excitedly.

"I don't get it," Stephanie said.

"We've been reading the clue wrong. I thought it meant that the treasure has been recovered, you know, like they have already retrieved it. But that doesn't make any sense."

"Why?" Stephanie persisted.

"Because the clue says "recovered *by* the darkness" instead of "recovered *from* the darkness". I think the clue means that he literally *re-covered* the gold. It's still here, just hidden from view."

"That makes sense," Stephanie said. "The clue does say the treasure remains where it was found."

"That's right," Catherine nodded. "It was found here, and it's still here. It's just covered up somehow."

We looked around the space again, carefully examining each wall.

"Hey, does this wall look a little shinier than the other ones?" I asked, shining my flashlight over the wall closest to the massive pile of boulders. I reached out and ran my hand over the wall. It was smooth, unlike the other walls, which were much rougher to the touch.

While the others examined the wall themselves, I reached for the rusted pickaxe leaning against the far wall.

"Watch out, I want to try something," I said, hefting the heavy tool over one shoulder. The others quickly cleared out of the way. I raised the pickaxe over my head, then brought it down with a loud thump against the wall. I half expected it to bounce off and hoped it wouldn't hit me in the head. Instead, the tip buried itself into the wall. I jiggled it back and forth and yanked it free. I looked at the wall, lit brightly by my friends' flashlights. Shining back was a streak of gold!

"He painted over the gold!" I exclaimed. "The treasure is still here, just painted over to make it look like coal."

"Just like the clue said," Catherine smiled. "He re-covered it."

I took a few more swings and revealed more gold.

"We did it!" Justin yelled. "We found the treasure."

"And what are you going to do about it?" a gruff voice asked.

We had been so busy high-fiving each other that we hadn't noticed the old man with the beard enter from the tunnel.

Chapter 20

We jumped at the sound of his voice. I reached for the pickaxe to use as a weapon, but he snatched it out of my hand and easily tossed the heavy tool across the tunnel, where it clanged noisily against the wall.

"Well?" he asked.

"Well what?" I asked, my voice catching in my throat. Catherine reached out and took Stephanie's hand for support. Justin's eyes darted left and right as if contemplating making a break for it.

"This is private property, you know. Do your parents know you're trespassing?

"We were just...just looking for something," Justin stammered.

"Treasure, right?"

"Yes, sir. And we found it! Now we can—" I started before I saw the look on the old man's face.

"Now you can what?" he asked angrily. "What makes you think it's yours to do anything with?"

"I know, but—"

"But nothing. It's not yours and that's the end of it! Now give me that satchel," the man demanded. Justin looked confused, then realized the old man was referring to his backpack.

The man yanked the backpack from Justin's hand. "Now the flashlights," he said.

We looked at each, fear dawning. Slowly, we handed him our lights. The cave grew steadily darker as, one by one, he flipped off the flashlights and stuffed them into the backpack.

"I bet you think you're all are pretty smart, don't you?" he snarled. "Well, let's see how smart you really are."

With that, he abruptly turned and receded into the tunnel, the light quickly fading until we were left in absolute darkness. I raised my hand in front of my face, but I couldn't see my wiggling fingers only an inch away. For a moment there was complete silence as the echoes of the man's retreat into the dark tunnel faded away.

"Okay, let's give him a couple of minutes to get down the tunnel," Catherine said quietly, breaking the silence.

"And then what?" I asked. "I'm not taking a step down that tunnel without a flashlight. One wrong step and we drop down into one of those pits."

"We don't need flashlights," Catherine said.

"Um, yeah, we do," Stephanie said, her voice quavering.

"Stephanie, put your hand on my shoulder." There was a shuffling noise as Stephanie moved toward Catherine's voice.

"Okay, Jordan, you're next. Put your hand on Stephanie's shoulder. And Justin, put your hand on Jordan's," Catherine said, her voice sounding very calm in the blackness.

When we had all joined, Catherine started to move slowly into the tunnel, the rest of us moving tentatively behind her.

"But how do you know you're not leading us the wrong way?" I asked.

"It was Justin's idea, so I'll let him tell you," said Catherine.

Justin's quiet chuckle sounded eerie in the darkness, but it somehow made me feel better to hear it.

"The string!" he said. "Catherine still has the string."

I had forgotten all about Justin's backup plan. All we had to do was follow the string and it would lead us all the way back to the coal chute. It was slow, but our little parade shuffled its way along as Catherine carefully followed the string.

At long last there was the clanging sound of Catherine's foot hitting metal. We had made it back!

"Now all we have to do is..." I started, but my voice trailed off when I heard a noise behind us. It sounded like someone in pain.

"Quiet, everyone," Stephanie said.

We listened and then heard the sound again. It was a quiet groan of pain.

"It must be the old man," Catherine said. "We have to help him."

"Why?" I asked. "He left us in the cave with no way out. Why should we help him now?"

A faint cry for help came out of the darkness.

"We could escape and send someone back in to help," Justin suggested.

"But he sounds like he needs someone now," Catherine countered.

"Catherine's right," Stephanie said. "We have to help."

This time Justin led the way as we slowly moved down the tunnel, following the sound of the old man's pleas for help. When we got close to the sound, Justin called out. "Hold on, we're almost there!"

"Be careful!" the old man called out. "There's a pit."

And that's when Justin fell.

Chapter 21

"Justin!" Catherine screamed.

"It's okay," he answered calmly. "I just tripped over my backpack. Hold on." Suddenly we were blinded as Justin turned on a flashlight.

We found the other flashlights and looked around. We were just a few feet short of a pit. Shining our lights into the hole, we saw the old man. He was holding one leg and grimacing.

"Are you okay?" Stephanie called down.

"My leg is a little cut up but I don't think it's broken," he said. "I don't think I can climb out though."

"I think we can help," Justin said. He reached into his backpack and pulled out a coil of rope. He lowered one end of the rope into the hole.

"Tie that around you, sir," he said.

When the rope was tightly secured around him, the four of us started to pull. I wasn't sure if we would be able to lift him, but with all of us pulling, it was easier than I thought. We had him out of the hole in less than a minute.

Justin gave the man a drink from a water bottle he pulled from a pocket of his backpack. Stephanie used one of the bandanas to wrap the cut on the man's leg.

"Do you think you'll be able to walk?" she asked.

"Yeah, I think so."

There was a long silence before the man finally spoke again.

"Why did you come back for me?" he asked.

"We couldn't just leave you down in that hole, could we?" Justin said.

"I don't know. After the way I treated you, I wouldn't have blamed you."

"He's got a point, you know," I said. We all laughed, including the old man.

"Well, we're just glad you're not seriously hurt," Catherine said.

"Can I ask you a question?" the old man said. "What would a bunch of kids do with a treasure?"

"We just want to get our math competition back," Stephanie said quietly.

The man looked confused. Stephanie went on to explain that the cuts to the school budget meant we wouldn't be able to compete in the math contest.

"A math competition, huh?"

Stephanie nodded. "You're Cletus Maynard, aren't you?"

A look of surprise came over the man's face. "Yeah. So you figured out who I was and how to find the treasure, huh? How'd you do that all by yourself?"

Stephanie shook her head. "It was all of us, sir. I found the clue in the book. It was a pigpen cipher, wasn't it?"

"Don't know anything about a pigpen cipher. My daddy always called it the Freemason's cipher."

"Anyway, Justin," she said, pointing at Justin, "showed us how to solve it. That led us to the chair in the library. We snuck in during one of the tours and I took a picture of the next clue."

"You're pretty smart, aren't you?" the old man asked.

"Not just me, Mr. Maynard. Catherine figured out the clue about seventy-nine meaning gold. Jordan put together the clue about Barry Goldwater. And Justin figured out the rescue tunnel started in the basement."

Throughout the explanation, the old man nodded thoughtfully.

"When I saw you reading that history book, I thought I'd have a little fun and leave you a little clue. I never thought you and your friends would be able to figure it out," he said.

"Wait, you didn't leave the clue back in 1984?" I asked.

"No, when your friend went up to talk to the librarian, I snuck over and wrote it."

Justin nodded. "I thought that might be the case. That explains why it was such a short clue and used such a simple cipher."

Cletus nodded. "I only had a minute or two, so it had to be quick."

"Have you been following us all over town?" Stephanie asked.

"I saw you copying down the clue from the book, and I wanted to see if you were getting anywhere with it. I was starting to get a little worried. If I'd ever thought there was any way you and your friends would be able to figure it out, I wouldn't have even left it. Then I saw you and your friends taking the tour of the house and figured you were getting closer when I saw you hiding in the library."

"Wait—you saw me in the library?" Stephanie asked. "But how…?"

"There are lots of secret passages in the house. I heard that my great-granddaddy loved secrets, and I guess I do too." He chuckled.

"So you're the reason people hear bumps in the wall sometimes?"

"I suppose I am."

We laughed. Not only had we found the treasure, but we had also figured out the mystery behind the ghost in the haunted house. It wasn't a ghost after all, just an old man visiting his home.

"But how do you get into the house?" I asked.

"Well, I used to do it the same way the girls did," he laughed. "Through the coal chute. I'm a little too old for that now, so I finally snuck a key from the tour guide and had a duplicate made.

"Mr. Maynard," Catherine said. "How come you disappeared all of those years ago?"

Cletus explained that he had been brokenhearted when his wife died and decided to leave Maynard. "Everything in the town reminded me of her, so I decided to just take off. I wandered around the country, doing part time work when I could, living off the land when there was no work to be found. I never stayed in one place for more than a month or so, then I was off again."

He explained that after being gone almost twenty years, he had hitched a ride with an over the road truck driver who dropped him off at the outskirts of Maynard.

"I almost didn't recognize the town," he said. "I couldn't believe how much it had grown since I had left. One thing hadn't changed a bit though; my old house still stood atop the highest hill on the north side of town. It looked like it hadn't aged a day. Since no one recognized me, I decided to stay for a while. I rented a small apartment on the outside of town, but I visit my old home quite a bit."

"You pay to take a tour of your own house?" I asked.

"No, can't say that I've ever paid for the tour," he said.

"You come in at night after the tours are over, don't you?" Catherine asked.

"It doesn't seem right for me to have to pay two bucks to visit my own house," Cletus smiled.

"Speaking of money..." Justin started, looking at Cletus.

"You want to know what's going to happen with the treasure, don't you?"

We looked at him anxiously.

"Give me a good reason why I shouldn't just keep it," he said.

"Your great-grandfather founded this town," I said. "If it wasn't for him, there wouldn't even be a Maynard."

"So?"

"So, he cared about the people here. He built the first library, didn't he?" I replied.

"And your grandfather and great-uncle used some of the treasure to keep the town going during the Depression, didn't they?" Stephanie added.

"The town was more like family back then," Cletus said, a far-off look in his eyes.

"Throughout the history of the town, it's been the Maynard family that kept it all together. Don't you want to continue the family tradition?" Justin asked.

Cletus looked each of us in the eyes, a thoughtful look on his face. At long last, he smiled. "Well, kids, I don't really have any need for treasure at my age, do I?"

Chapter 22

The Mayor and town council looked surprised to see four kids approach the microphone during the public comments portion of the town meeting.

"I'm usually glad to see youth participating in government," the mayor said, "but this probably isn't the best time."

I started to interrupt, but the mayor continued. "We've got some serious financial issues we're working through, so I'd like to hear from some of the adults in the room."

"Are you saying you don't want to hear from us even if we have a solution to your problem?" I asked.

The mayor looked skeptical. Mr. Seyhorn, the town attorney, scowled from the far end of the long table stretching across the front of the room. "You kids think you have a solution, do you?" he asked sarcastically. "What do you want to do, some kind of bake sale?"

"We were thinking something more along the lines of a gold mine," Justin said, doing everything he could to keep the smirk from his face.

"Kind of beats a bake sale, doesn't it?" Stephanie said, her voice sweet yet dripping with sarcasm.

"I find it hard to believe you've found a gold mine," Mr. Seyhorn said, his mouth pinched into a frown. "Can we move on, Mr. Mayor?"

"If I may address the council?" came a voice from behind us.

"And who are you, sir?" asked the mayor.

"I'm Cletus Maynard."

There was a loud gasp from the room, and the noise increased tenfold as everyone wanted to know if the man was really who he said he was. It was several minutes before the mayor was able to settle the crowd down.

"You're Cletus Maynard, huh?" the mayor asked. Cletus nodded.

"And where do you live, sir?"

"Well, unofficially I guess I live at the Maynard House," Cletus answered with a slight smile. The crowd erupted again.

"And what do you know about this nonsense of a bunch of kids finding a gold mine?" Mr. Seyhorn asked.

"They didn't find a gold mine," Cletus answered.

"That's what I thought."

"I mean, technically, it was my grandfather who found the gold. The kids did do a great job of re-finding it though."

Once again, the crowd had to be admonished to be silent.

"Let's assume for a moment that there is gold," Mr. Seyhorn said.

"That's not an assumption!" I chimed in, drawing a stern face from the attorney.

"Again, assuming there is gold, what do you intend to do with it, sir?"

"That depends on the town council," Stephanie said.

The mayor raised an eyebrow in amusement but let her continue.

"We have several requests, Mr. Mayor," Stephanie said. "First, Mr. Maynard will be allowed to live in the mansion."

"Absolutely not," said Mrs. Middleton, one of the other members of the town council. "The house belongs to the town."

"Actually, Mr. Maynard rightfully owns the house and the land," Justin said. "And, I should add, that would include the gold."

"The house was forfeited when Mr. Maynard deserted the town," Mr. Seyhorn replied smugly. "You'll learn this when you get a little older son, but when you don't pay your property taxes, you give up your rights to your property."

"He's right, Justin," said Cletus.

The attorney gave us one of those I-told-you-so looks and crossed his arms.

"Unless, of course, you are granted a permanent waiver on those property taxes," Cletus continued, pulling a yellowed sheet of paper from his jacket pocket. "It turns out the town was pretty thankful when my great-granddaddy built them a library."

The attorney looked over the document. After reading it, he looked over at the mayor and nodded.

"It turns out the young man makes a good point about the owner of the property," the mayor said. "Any objections to allowing Mr. Maynard to live in his own house?" There were none.

"And we have one more condition," Catherine said.

"And that is?" the mayor asked.

"Mr. Maynard would like a job."

"What kind of a job? Is he qualified?"

"Oh, I'm sure he's more than qualified," Catherine smiled slyly. "He'd like to be a tour guide at the Maynard mansion."

"I don't think you'll find anyone who knows the history of Maynard better than he does," Justin added.

"And there's one more benefit," I chimed in. "You

should be able to raise the price of the tours to five dollars."

"Do you really think anyone is going to pay that much for a tour of an old house?" the mayor asked doubtfully.

"I know I would if the tour included some of the secret passageways hidden throughout the mansion," I answered. The crowd erupted again, and this time the mayor didn't even attempt to silence them.

It was several days before a mining team could be brought in to assess the worth of the gold deposit. It turned out there was enough gold in those rocks to cover the town's financial shortfall for many years to come. There was a big ceremony in the town square, where the mayor announced the good news. The Math Kids were recognized for finding the treasure. The mayor even gave us the key to the city, although none of us had any idea what we were going to do with a giant key.

From our spot on the stage, we could see our friends, our beaming parents, and a great many other townspeople. In the back of the crowd, we could just make out Cletus Maynard leaning against a decorative light pole. When the festivities were over, the four of us made our way through the happy crowd to find him.

"Way to go, kids," he said with a smile.

"We couldn't have done it without you, Mr. Maynard," I said.

"Please, call me Cletus," he responded. "I'm just happy that the town is back on a solid financial footing again."

"It was awfully nice of you to give away your money, Cletus."

"I'm just happy I was able to help. My great-grandfather founded this town. I think he would be proud of me, and that's all I need."

We thought about that for a moment, and then Stephanie handed over the key to the city. Cletus took it with a smile, but I could see tears forming in the corners of his eyes.

"We're proud of you too, Cletus," she said.

"And I owe you some thanks," he said. "If it wasn't for you, I wouldn't have the best job in the world."

As for us, we were just happy to know that our competition against the other fourth-grade students would go on as planned, even though it had been pushed until the Saturday after school was over. We were ready to get back into the classroom and resume practicing. We didn't have much time, and the Math Kids needed to get back to what we did best—math.

Chapter 23

Only a week until the competition, and Mrs. Gouche was really piling it on. We were coming into school forty-five minutes early to practice. We worked math problems over lunch. We stayed for an hour after school. And still we worried it wasn't enough.

"You're doing great," our teacher reassured us, but it didn't convince us. No matter how many problems we were able to solve correctly, it seemed there were more we couldn't figure out. The tension was growing, and we were starting to get on each other's nerves.

"No, Justin, that isn't right!" I snapped one afternoon after school when he wasted twenty minutes trying to take us down the wrong path on a difficult problem. He looked hurt but didn't respond. Catherine and Stephanie just looked at each other.

"Maybe we should call it early today, guys," Stephanie said diplomatically. "We've been working hard all week. Maybe an evening off would do us all some good."

I started to protest, but realized she was probably right. It wasn't like me to get mad at my best friend, especially when it came to math. Catherine was gathering up the scrap paper for the recycling bin, taking a quick glance through each sheet to see if it was something we needed to save for future reference. Stephanie was cleaning the whiteboard, so that left Justin and I alone.

"Sorry, man," I said, breaking the uncomfortable silence.

"No, I'm sorry," he responded. "I was taking us the wrong direction."

"Yeah, well, that's going to happen sometime. I do it all the time."

"Yeah, you do," Justin said with a smile. I grinned, relieved that we were able to get past the awkward moment.

Justin noticed Stephanie and Catherine were standing by the door with their backpacks and looked at the clock.

"Hey, slackers, it's only four-fifteen," he said. "Old Mike won't throw us out for another twenty minutes or so. What do you think, one more problem?"

The girls looked at each other and smiled. "We're in," Catherine said, dropping her backpack on the nearest chair.

"Okay, I've got one," I said, looking through a list of problems Mrs. Gouche had provided. "If you add an 8 to the right side of a two-digit number, the value of the new three-digit number is 386 more than the two-digit number. What is the two-digit number?"

Wait! Do you want to try to solve this puzzle before seeing if the Math Kids can do it? Start with a two-digit number *ab*. If you add an 8 to the right side to make a three-digit number *ab8*, the new three-digit number is 386 more than the original number. What is the original number? Good luck!

You could see Justin's eyes light up as soon as I finished reading the question. He loved math problems like this.

"Okay, where should we start?" he asked.

We waited because we knew he already had an idea for how he wanted to start.

"v, I've got an idea," he said after a few seconds. He went to the whiteboard to write down his thoughts.

"We start with a number *ab*, where *a* is the first digit and *b* is the second, right?" he said, writing *ab* on the board. "But we know this really means ten times *a* plus *b*, because *a* is in the tens column." He erased *ab* and replaced it with $10a + b$.

"So, when we add 8 to the end of the number, we get 10 times *a* plus *b* plus 8, right?" I asked.

Stephanie shook her head. "I don't think that's right, Jordan," she said. "If we add the 8 to the end, then the *a* moves to the hundreds column and the *b* to the tens column."

She went to the board and wrote $100a + 10b + 8$.

"That's our three-digit number," she said, then asked, "Does everyone agree?"

We all nodded in agreement. Now we were getting somewhere.

"And we know this new number is equal to the original number plus 386," Catherine said.

Stephanie added this new information to the board.

$$100a + 10b + 8 = 10a + b + 386$$

Now we just needed to solve that equation. We subtracted 10a from both sides, because we knew that as long as we did the same thing to both sides of the equal sign, the sides would still be equal. Stephanie wrote the new equation on the board.

$$90a + 10b + 8 = b + 386$$

We did the same thing with the *b*'s, subtracting them from both sides.

$$90a + 9b + 8 = 386$$

Finally, we subtracted 8 from both sides.

$$90a + 9b = 378$$

And that's where we got stuck. We thought about just plugging in numbers for *a* and *b* to see if we could come up with an answer that worked, but I knew that this guessing method always bothered Justin. He hated it when he could only solve a problem by trial and error.

It was Catherine who figured out the step that solved the problem.

"What if we divided both sides of the equation by 9?" she asked.

As it turns out, that was exactly what we needed to do. When we divided both sides by 9, we were left with $10a + b = 42$.

"That's it!" I shouted.

"But don't we still need to figure out what *a* and *b* are?" Justin asked.

"$10a + b$ is our original two-digit number, so we've already solved it! The number we're looking for is 42."

Even though we were sure we had solved it correctly, we checked our work just in case.

"If we start with 42 and then add an 8 to the end, we get 428," Stephanie said. "And 428 is equal to 42 plus 386."

The Math Kids strike again! We had solved another of Mrs. Gouche's puzzles. With four days to go, maybe we had a chance at winning the district math tournament after all.

Chapter 24

The morning of the district math tournament was rainy with gusty winds. The competition was being held in the gymnasium at Maynard High School. We managed to make it to the gym door without getting too wet, and we waved at my mom as she drove away. Justin tugged on the door.

It was locked.

We were completely soaked by the time we made it back around to the front of the school and in through the main door. Puddles formed under us as the water continued to drip off our sodden clothes. I hoped our early bad luck was not an omen for things to come.

We stopped off in the restroom to use paper towels to dry ourselves as much as we could, but we were still damp when we got to the gym. The five other teams had already assembled at their tables, so I took the opportunity to have a look at the competition. Two of the teams—Armstrong and Twillman—looked very confident, joking around as they waited for the competition to start. The other three teams—Wright, Maynard, and Eastman—were milling around anxiously. I shared their sentiments. We looked around the tables and saw McNair Elementary printed on a tent-card, so we made our way to the table and sat down.

"You ready to do this?" I asked my friends.

"You bet!" Justin said. Stephanie and Catherine nodded, but I could tell they were nervous. I was too. I just wanted to get it started so I didn't have to think about it anymore. Luckily, we didn't have to wait long.

"Can I have your attention, please?" came a loud voice over the speakers. "I'm Mr. Trudeau, the head of the math department here at the high school. I want to welcome all of you to the fourth-grade district math competition. You've already won at your individual schools, so you're already champions in my book. Give yourselves a big hand!"

This was answered with sporadic clapping from the fourth-grade teams.

"Come on, you can do better than that!"

The applause was louder and more sustained this time.

"That's better," he smiled. "Okay, let's get started. There will be two rounds in the competition. The first round will be team problem-solving. The top two teams in round one will compete in the head-to-head round for the district championship."

He had a few more words to say, but I wasn't really listening anymore. After months of preparation, it was time to get going, so I was happy when the judges began handing out the question sheets for the team problem-solving round.

We had one hour to solve ten problems. We had decided ahead of time to split into teams of two for the problems. Justin and I would start with problem one and Stephanie and Catherine would begin with problem six. If either pair finished their five problems before time was up, they would help the other two with their remaining problems.

Justin and I breezed through problem one.

> *Ann is three times as old as Beth. In twelve years, Ann will only be twice as old as Beth. How old is Ann today?*

HEY! IF YOU WANT TO TRY THE DISTRICT MATH COMPETITION QUESTIONS, YOU CAN FIND THEM (AND HINTS ON HOW TO SOLVE THEM) IN THE APPENDIX AT THE END OF THE BOOK.

The second question was tougher and took a much longer time to solve.

You won a contest. You have the option of taking one of the following prizes:

1) *$1,000,000*
2) *1 penny today. 2 pennies tomorrow and double the number of pennies every day for 30 days.*

   Which prize would give you the most money?

At first glance, it looked obvious—take the million dollars! But we decided we'd better work out the math just to make sure. Sure enough, doubling the pennies ended up giving us more than ten million dollars. We were happy to get the right answer but dismayed by the amount of time it took us to work through the math. I glanced at the clock—less than thirty minutes to go and we were only on problem three.

Luckily, problem three was easier.

East Town and West Town are 260 miles apart. One train leaves East Town traveling 70 miles per hour. Another train leaves West Town traveling 60 miles per hour. When will the two trains meet? How far from East Town will they be when they meet?

We quickly figured out that the trains would meet in 2 hours and would be 140 miles from East Town when they met.

Another look at the clock showed sixteen minutes remained.

"How are you two doing?" I whispered over to Stephanie.

"Four down, one to go," she answered. "But we're not sure of our answer on problem eight."

I quickly did the math in my head. Between us, we had completed seven problems, but were only confident on six of them. We needed to hurry if we were going to get finished.

And hurry we did. Problem four was another easy one, luckily.

> *Sue has 11 more nickels than quarters. If she has $2.65 altogether, how many coins does she have?*

Only one more problem to go to finish up our five, but we were down to only seven minutes. Justin and I worked furiously, but we couldn't solve the last problem before time was up. Stephanie and Catherine were stumped with their final problem too, so we ended up with eight completed problems.

That wasn't the end of the bad news though. Stephanie and Catherine got one of their problems wrong. They were close but missed a key piece of data in their calculations. Justin and I also missed problem four. We figured out that there were seven quarters and eighteen nickels, but the problem asked for the total number of coins. We missed the last simple step of adding the number of nickels and quarters together to get the answer of twenty-five.

That left us with six correct answers out of ten. Would that be enough to get us into the final round? We waited anxiously while the judges continued to look through all the answers. Stephanie was tugging at her ponytail while I chewed nervously on my fingernails. Catherine was absently doodling on her sketchpad. Justin was the only one who seemed calm, but I knew my friend well enough to know that he was kicking himself for missing that fourth question. He was always so detailed when he worked on a problem, so to get it right but miss that final key step was something he'll probably think about for a long time.

"Okay, we've got the results of the problem-solving," Mr. Trudeau finally said. The room grew silent in anticipation. He looked down at the piece of paper he held in his hand. "The top two teams will be going on to compete in the head-to-head round."

He glanced at the results again. "These were really tough questions, and every team did very well. The top team—Armstrong Elementary—got eight correct answers."

My heart sank. If they got eight right, there was no way our six correct answers were going to be good enough to get us into the head-to-head round.

"Well, we gave it a good shot, guys," I said. Justin didn't look up, his eyes fixed on the floor. I looked at Stephanie and Catherine, and their body language said it all. We had tried, but...

"And the second-place team, with six correct answers, is McNair Elementary," Mr. Trudeau said.

I couldn't believe my ears. Had we really made it into the final round?

We didn't have long to take it in. The judges herded us to one of the two tables set up for the head-to-head competition. I looked across at the team from Armstrong. They were dressed in identical light blue shirts with their team name—the Mathketeers—and a logo with four crossed swords. I grinned, remembering that the Mathketeers was my original idea for our own math club name and how Stephanie had said she was glad we hadn't picked something cutesy.

"Remember, the first team to correctly answer seven questions will be the fourth-grade district math champions," Mr. Trudeau said. "Math Kids, are you ready?"

"Yes, sir," I answered for the team.

"Mathketeers, are you ready?"

"One for all, and all for one!" a tall boy with blond hair shouted, drawing a laugh from the small crowd. I wished we had come up with something clever for our response.

And then the questions began. Nine questions later, it was over.

We got off to a good start when Justin correctly answered a probability question. Then Armstrong reeled off the next six answers. We were shocked by the speed in which they answered. Stephanie kept us in the game by barely beating the Armstrong team to the buzzer for question eight. Her voice was shaking, but her answer was correct. That bought us one more question, which the tall blond boy answered quickly and correctly.

And just like that, the head-to-head round, and the competition, was over. The Armstrong team had won. We shook their hands and returned to our table quietly.

"Congratulations to the team from Armstrong Elementary," said Mr. Trudeau. "Accepting the first-place trophy will be Josh Benson."

The tall boy rose gracefully and went to the podium to receive the trophy while the crowd clapped politely. He whispered something to Mr. Trudeau, who smiled and nodded.

"Mr. Benson would like to say a few words," he said before stepping aside from the podium.

"First of all, I want to thank my teammates, Becky, Scott, and Tonya. Great job, guys! Second, I want to thank our teacher, Mrs. Jackson, who spent so much time with us in preparing for this competition. Finally, I want to thank the Math Kids from McNair Elementary."

I looked up in surprise.

"If it weren't for their math and detective skills, none of us would even be here today. Let's give them a big round of applause!"

The room erupted in loud clapping and cheering. We rose to acknowledge the ovation. Stephanie and Catherine had ear-to-ear smiles, and Justin was positively beaming. I just took it all in. We had finished in second place, but it felt more like we had won. One thought filled my head: *We'll be back next year, and you'd better watch out!*

The End

Appendix

Was The Mine Disaster In The Book Based On A Real Event?

No, but there were a lot of mine disasters in the early 1900s. The Monongah Mining Disaster was called "the worst in American history." On December 6, 1907, there was an explosion in a mine. At least 362 men were killed, but it was probably higher since many workers took their children and other relatives into the mine. The explosion was probably caused when an electrical spark or lamp flame ignited either methane gas or coal dust. Most of the miners died instantly in the explosion, but some may have suffocated to death. The blast caused extensive damage to the mine and destroyed the ventilation systems which provided oxygen to the mines.

Only five people were rescued after the explosion.

In 1910, Congress created the United States Bureau of Mines to investigate and inspect mines to reduce explosions.

Finding The Coin That Is Different

There are lots of math puzzles involving finding out which object is different using a scale. In the book, the Math Kids solved the following puzzle:

Someone tried to pay you with twelve gold coins. You learned that one of the coins is fake. It looks identical, but it is just a little heavier than the others. You have a balance scale. Can you find the fake coin using the scale only three times?

They were able to solve this problem, but then Mrs. Gauche asked if they could solve the same problem if they didn't know if the coin was heavier or lighter. This makes the problem more difficult, because if one side of the scale is heavier, we don't know if the heavy side has a heavy coin or if the light side has a light coin.

Let's start by numbering the coins from 1 to 12 to make it easier to keep track of them.

Weighing 1—Weigh 1, 2, 3, 4 against 5, 6, 7, 8

A) If the two sides balance, the bad coin is in the group 9, 10, 11, 12.

Weighing 2—Weigh coins 1, 2 against coins 11, 12 (because we now know coins 1 and 2 are good coins)

a) If the two sides balance, the bad coin is either 9 or 10

Weighing 3—Weigh coin 1 against coin 9 (because we know that coin 1 is a good coin)

i) If the two sides balance, that means coin 10 is the bad coin

ii) If the two sides don't balance, then coin 9 is the bad coin

b) If the two sides don't balance, the bad coin is either 11 or 12

Weighing 3—Weigh coin 1 against coin 11 (because we know coin 1 is good)

i) If the two sides balance, that means coin 12 is the bad coin

ii) If the two sides don't balance, then coin 11 is the bad coin

B) If the two sides don't balance, the bad coin is one of the eight coins on the scale. Let's say 5, 6, 7, 8 is the heavy side.

Weighing 2—Weigh coins 1, 5, 6 against coins 2, 7, 8

a) If the two sides balance, the bad coin is either 3 or 4.

Weighing 3—Weigh coin 3 against coin 9

i) If the sides balance, 4 is the bad coin.
ii) If the sides don't balance, 3 is the bad coin.

b) If the two sides don't balance, and side 2, 7, 8 is the heavy side, either 7 or 8 is the bad coin (and is heavy) or 1 is the bad coin (and is light)

Weighing 3—Weigh coin 7 against coin 8

i) If they don't balance, the heavy side has the bad coin.
ii) If the sides balance, 1 is the bad coin.

c) If the two sides don't balance, and side 1, 5, 6 is the heavy side, either 5 or 6 is the bad coin (and is heavy) or 2 is the bad coin (and is light)

Weighing 3—Weigh coin 5 against coin 6

i) If they don't balance, the heavy side has the bad coin.

ii) If the sides balance, 2 is the bad coin.

Wow! Not knowing whether the bad coin is heavier or lighter sure makes the problem tougher, doesn't it?

Letter Frequency

The Math Kids used letter frequency to help solve the riddle left by Cletus Maynard. Letter frequency is the amount of times letters appear on average in written language. Since vowels (*A*, *E*, *I*, *O*, and *U*) are in almost every word, we would expect these letters to appear more often than letters like *Q* and *Z*. The method was formalized by Al-Kindi, an Arab mathematician, about twelve hundred years ago, but it could have been used all the way back to the time of Julius Caeser.

Knowing the frequency of each letter helped early typesetters to figure out how many of each metal letter they would need to print a page of type. It also influenced the design of typewriter keyboards. The more frequently used letters are easy to reach, while letters like *Q* and *Z* are a further reach.

A letter having a high frequency doesn't mean there will be an exact number of that letter in a message. Sometimes short messages will not follow the pattern. In longer messages the letter frequency will get closer and closer to the "normal" frequency, although in 1939, Earnest Vincent Wright wrote a 50,000 word novel called Gadsby which did not include the letter *E*!

The Enigma Machine

The Enigma machine was a famous data encryption machine used by the Germans during World War II to send secret messages. An Enigma machine allows a message to be encrypted in billions of ways, making it almost impossible for someone to crack the code.

In a simple Caesar cipher, the letters in the alphabet are shifted by some fixed number of spaces. In an Enigma machine, the mechanical rotors caused the number of spaces to change every time a letter was entered, changing the entire encoding scheme. This means that an *A* might be encoded as a *B*, the next *A* as an *M*, the next *A* as an *F*, and so on. Using letter frequency analysis would no longer work to decode the message, making the cipher very difficult to solve without having another Enigma machine and the same settings for the rotors.

The first level of encoding was a plugboard on the keyboard that allowed you to switch ten pairs of letters. If you switched the *A* and the *P*, for example, the word *PAPER* would be encoded as *APAER*.

The second level of encoding was the mechanical rotors. The Enigma machine used three rotors, but the Germans had five different rotors to pick from, and they could place them in any order. For the first rotor, there were five different choices that could be chosen. For the second rotor, there would be four, and for the third rotor, there would be three. That meant there were $5 \times 4 \times 3 = 60$ possible rotor configurations that could be used.

The third level of encoding was setting the starting position for each of the twenty-six letters on each rotor. Since each rotor had twenty-six letters, there were $26 \times 26 \times 26 = 17{,}576$ different starting letter combinations.

Altogether, there were 158,962,555,217,826,360,000 different ways to set up the Enigma machine! If you like large numbers, that's almost 159 *quintillion*.

So how was the Enigma code cracked? It turns out there were a couple flaws in the Enigma machine and how the messages were encrypted. First, the machine would not let a letter be encoded to itself, meaning an *M* could never be encoded as an *M*. That reduced the number of potential combinations. Also, the allies learned that each message usually contained a weather report and almost always ended with *Heil Hitler*. Alan Turing and Gordon Welchman took advantage of these flaws and built a machine called a bombe that used electric circuits to solve the codes very quickly. Using multiple machines, they were able to decode more than three thousand messages a day.

What Is The Periodic Table Of Elements?

The periodic table is a way to arrange the chemical elements by the number of protons the element has (the atomic number), the number of electron orbits, and the element's chemical properties.

The rows are called periods and the columns are called groups (or families). All the elements in a period have the same number of electron orbits. All the elements in a group have similar chemical behaviors. For example, copper (Cu), silver (Ag), and gold (Au) are all metals that transmit electricity very well.

Dmitri Mendeleev, a Russian chemist, made the first periodic table in 1869. The periodic chart is used in chemistry, nuclear physics, and other sciences.

(View The Periodic Table Of Elements on page 76–77)

How Is Math Used In Data Encryption?

The Math Kids used math in the book to help them figure out the encryption by knowing that some letters appear more often than others when we write. But math is even more important than that when we use encryption on the internet.

Lots of people buy things on the internet. Others do online banking. Still others send private messages. How are the messages kept secret from bad people who may intercept them on the way?

Here's an example of how encryption works. Let's say Catherine wants to send a box of cookies to Stephanie. Robbie says he'll take the box to her. Catherine is worried Robbie will eat the cookies, so she puts a lock on the box.

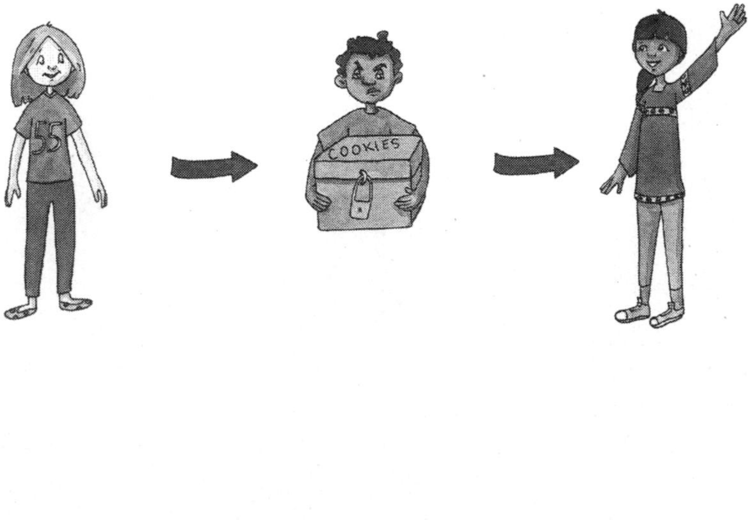

Robbie can't get to the cookies, so they remain safe. Unfortunately, Stephanie can't open the box, either. Stephanie puts her own lock on the box and sends it back to Catherine. Once again, Robbie can't get to the cookies.

Now Catherine takes off her lock (she can do this because she has the key) and sends the box back to Stephanie. Robbie can't get to the cookies because the box still has Stephanie's lock on it.

When the box of cookies gets back to Stephanie, she removes her lock (she can do this because she has the key) and enjoys the delicious box of cookies.

But what does this have to do with math? When we send data over the internet, we can use math to put on electronic "locks."

Let's say Catherine wants to send the message 24680 to Stephanie without Robbie being able to read the message. Catherine has a "key" that only she knows. Let's say her key is 12345. Before sending her message to Stephanie, she adds her key to the message. So, instead of sending the message 24680, she sends the message 36925 (24680 + 12345).

When Stephanie gets the message, she adds her own "lock." Her key is 67890, so she adds this to Catherine's message. She sends the message 104915 (36925 + 67890) to Catherine.

When Catherine gets Stephanie's message, she "unlocks her lock" by subtracting her key. She sends 92570 (104915 - 12345) to Stephanie.

When Stephanie receives it, she "unlocks" it by subtracting her own key. Now she can see Catherine's message of 24680 (92570 - 67890).

Robbie can't read the original message because the message always has a lock on it, so the message is secure.

Of course, the keys used for encryption on the internet are much more complicated than our example of simply adding a number. One way is to use two very large prime numbers as keys because it is very difficult for a computer to factor very large numbers.

District Math Competition Questions

1) *Ann is three times as old as Beth. In twelve years, Ann will only be twice as old as Beth. How old is Ann today?*

Hint:

One way to solve an age problem is to use variables (like a letter) to represent the ages. For example, we could use *A* for Ann's age and *B* for Beth's age. Then, when we say Ann is three times as old as Beth, we could write this as $A = 3B$.

How can we represent Ann's age in twelve years?

Solution:

$A = 3B$	Ann is three times as old as Beth
$A + 12 = 2(B + 12)$	Ann will be twice as old as Beth in 12 years
$3B + 12 = 2(B + 12)$	Since we know $A = 3B$, we can substitute this into the second equation
$3B + 12 = 2B + 24$	Do the multiplication in the parenthesis
$B + 12 = 24$	Subtract 2B from both sides of the equation
$B = 12$	Subtract 12 from both sides of the equation

This means Beth is 12 years old today. But the question is how old Ann is today. Remember that Ann is 3 times as old as Beth is, so we can just multiply by 3 to get Ann's age of 36.

Let's check our answer to make sure it's right:

Ann is 3 times as old as Beth ($36 = 3 \times 12$). That works!

In 12 years, Ann will be 48 ($36 + 12$) and Beth will be 24 ($12 + 12$), at which point Ann will be twice as old as Beth ($48 = 2 \times 24$). That works too, so we know we got the correct answer.

2) *You won a contest. You have the option of taking one of the following prizes:*
   i) *$1,000,000*
   ii) *1 penny today, 2 pennies tomorrow, and double the number of pennies every day for 30 days.*

Which prize would give you the most money?

Hint:

One way to solve this problem is to just do the math.

Day	Number of Pennies	Total
1	1	$ 0.01
2	2	$ 0.03
3	4	$ 0.07
4	8	$ 0.15
...	...	...

But Justin and Jordan knew this would take too long, so they looked for a pattern in the numbers. See if you can find a pattern between the day number and the total amount of money they have.

Solution:

Since they knew they were doubling the number of pennies every day, they looked for multiples of two.

Notice that the total number of pennies after day 2 is 3. Jordan thought the pattern might be $2^2 - 1 = 3$.

Note: 2^2 means two to the second power, which means 2×2.

But, if this is really the pattern, it must work for all other numbers too.

That means, for day 3, the number of pennies at the end of the day would have to be $2^3 - 1$, which is $(2 \times 2 \times 2) - 1$, which equals 7. That checks out.

For day 4, the number of pennies would be $2^4 - 1 = 16 - 1 = 15$. That one also works, so it looks like we found the pattern.

So, how many pennies would we have on day 30? According to our pattern, it would be $2^{30} - 1$. They had to use a calculator on this one, but they found that $2^{30} - 1 = 1{,}073{,}741{,}843$ pennies. They had to divide this by 100 since there are 100 pennies in a dollar. That gave them $10,737,418.23. Wow—that's almost 11 million dollars!

3) *East Town and West Town are 260 miles apart. One train leaves East Town traveling 70 miles per hour. Another train leaves West Town traveling 60 miles per hour. When will the two trains meet? How far from East Town will they be when they meet?*

Hint:
How quickly are the trains traveling toward each other? To figure this out, you must add the two train speeds together. Knowing how far apart they started, how long will it take for them to meet?

Solution:
The two trains are traveling 130 miles per hour (60 + 70) toward each other. Since they started 260 miles apart, it will take 2 hours for them to meet (260 ÷ 130). That answers first part of the question. The second part is how far will they be from East Town when they meet. Since the train from East Town is traveling at 70 miles per hour, it will travel 140 miles (70 mph × 2 hours) from East Town.

4) *Sue has 11 more nickels than quarters. If she has \$2.65 altogether, how many coins does she have?*

Hint:

Like the ages problem, it helps if we give the coins letter names. Let's use *Q* for the number of quarters and *N* for the number of nickels. Using these variable names, how would you write "there are 11 more nickels than quarters"? How would you write "the value of the nickels and quarters is \$2.65"?

Solution:

$N = Q + 11$	There are 11 more nickels than quarters
$5N + 25Q = 265$	Each nickel is 5 cents and each quarter 25 cents, so this is how we write the value of all the coins equals \$2.65 (265 cents)
$5(Q + 11) + 25Q = 265$	Replace N with Q + 11 from the first equation
$5Q + 55 + 25Q = 265$	Do the multiplication in the parenthesis
$30Q + 55 = 265$	Add the Q's together
$30Q = 210$	Subtract 55 from both sides
$Q = 7$	Divide both sides by 30

This means we have 7 quarters. We know that we have 11 more nickels than quarters, so we must have 18 nickels.

We've solved the problem! Or have we? Remember that the question asks how many coins Sue has. To get this, we must add the number of quarters and the number of nickels together to get 25 total coins.

Be very careful to make sure you are answering the question that was asked!

Coming Next!

An Incorrect Solution

*Book 5 in **The Math Kids** Series*

by

David Cole

Chapter 1

Low, dark clouds spit angry drops of rain onto the pavement, where they splattered into growing puddles of muddy water. Justin Grant kept his head down and plodded on toward school, trying to keep up with the much longer stride of Jordan Waters, his best friend since kindergarten.

Truth be told, neither was in much of a hurry to get to McNair Elementary. That was unusual, because both were good students and normally loved school, especially since they had formed the Math Kids club with Stephanie Lewis. The three had solved the mystery of the neighborhood burglars, but the club became complete when they had added Catherine Duchesne. With their new club member, they had solved the mystery of a bank robbery and found a fortune in gold that had helped the town recover from financial hardship. They had also come in second in the district math competition.

But that was all in fourth grade. Now they were

moving to fifth grade and things were changing—and not for the better.

For one thing, Catherine and Stephanie were going to be in a different classroom. The girls were going to be in Mrs. Wilson's class while the boys were going to be in Mr. Miller's room. His nickname was "Miller the killer" because he was so hard on kids. Some of the kids thought their fourth-grade teacher, Mrs. Gouche, had been tough too—they had called her Mrs. Grouch when she was mad—but the word was that Mr. Miller was much, much worse.

But that wasn't what was bothering Jordan about their new teacher. It was math. Mr. Miller hated math. He had the only classroom in the entire school who didn't have a math team in the school competition. Mr. Miller loved English and social studies but made it clear that math was his least favorite subject. Jordan did great in math, but he struggled with English. He hated to read, mixed up letters when he tried to spell, and couldn't stand to write papers. Mr. Miller was going to be his worst nightmare.

"This is going to be a lousy year, isn't it?" Jordan said to Justin as he used his long legs to step over a puddle in a low spot in the sidewalk.

"Yeah," replied Justin glumly. He didn't even bother to try to step over the puddle. He was one of the shortest kids in his grade and he knew his short legs weren't going to reach from one side to the other. He just plowed through the puddle, splashing water everywhere. He was glad he had worn an old pair of tennis shoes and not the new ones his mom had bought him.

"It's going to stink not having Stephanie and Catherine in the same class," Justin said as he shook water from one leg.

"Wouldn't really matter, since Mr. Miller hates math anyway," Jordan said. "I heard he doesn't even have math groups."

Justin didn't reply, just trudged through the rain in his soaked sneakers. The first day of fifth grade was already miserable and they hadn't even reached the school.

Four blocks away, Stephanie ducked her head and raced down the sidewalk and into the waiting dryness of Catherine's dad's car.

"Thanks so much for driving us to school, Mr. Duchesne," Stephanie said politely, shaking a few drops of water out of her ponytail onto the floor in the back seat.

"Happy to do it," Mr. Duchesne answered. "It's right on my way to the college anyway, so it's really no trouble. Besides, I still owe you one, don't I?"

Stephanie smiled as she remembered meeting Catherine and working with the Math Kids to solve the cryptic message Mr. Duchesne had left his daughter after he had been kidnapped. Teamwork and their math skills had helped them to rescue their new friend's father.

Mr. Duchesne taught math at the college and had a whole library of math books, some of which he had written himself. *Catherine is so lucky*, Stephanie thought to herself. She placed her gym bag on the seat next to her. If the rain stopped in time, maybe her soccer team would still be able to practice after school. Soccer was one of the few things in the world that Stephanie liked as much as math—well, almost as much. Catherine looked longingly at the bag containing Stephanie's soccer shorts, T-shirt, and sneakers. *I wish I could play soccer like Stephanie*, she thought.

"I can't believe they split us up into two different classrooms," Stephanie said.

"Yeah, it really stinks. Does that mean we'll have to be on a different math team for the district competition?"

"Worse. It means we'll actually have to compete against them in the school contest," Stephanie said gloomily.

"We'll beat them, of course, but it won't be nearly as much fun," Catherine said.

Catherine smiled to show she was only joking, but Stephanie was worried. Would this be the end of the Math Kids?

Acknowledgements

As I write this, the world is in the middle of a global pandemic. We're stuck in our homes, wearing masks in public, and missing too many opportunities to spend time with friends and loved ones. It reminds me that writing is a solitary endeavor for the most part. We write in a void, not knowing how our work is going to be received until many months later. What keeps me going is the encouragement I get from some of my loyal readers. Let me give you a few examples:

Ally and Vivie Clark, maybe the cutest twins on the planet, asked their dad if they could do a videoconference with me to ask me questions about my books. How cool is that? We did it and I had a ball answering their questions.

Jessica and Steve Gury asked if I could autograph some Math Kids books for birthday presents. They follow the Math Kids Facebook page and always provide encouraging words. Thanks!

Ethan Wickenhauser asked if he could get a

picture with me for his literary fair project. He said it would add “a special touch.” I can’t tell you how flattering that was to hear, Ethan.

There are others, people who have contacted me for autographed copies of the books, written reviews, come to one of my book signings, or reached out to me to say their kids really enjoyed the books. It’s those touch points that keep a writer going, and I want you all to know I appreciate it!

Thanks, as always, to Common Deer Press for publishing these books. I appreciate Kirsten and her team for making sure the content makes sense and the grammar and spelling don’t embarrass me. It’s a team effort and your work does not go unnoticed.

Shannon O’Toole’s illustrations are always a delight. I’m always excited to see what she comes up with and love that she continues to work with me on these books.

Thanks to my daughter Stephanie, who is a doctor, and her husband Andrew, who is a paramedic. I want you both to know how much I appreciate you being on the front lines in protecting us. Please stay safe!

Thanks to my son Justin for keeping me grounded. He has a knack for letting me know all the things I don’t know. Trust me—I need that.

Thanks to my son Jordan for the twenty hugs he gives me every single day. Each one is equally special.

And finally, thanks to my wife Debbie for ignoring the times I pretend to listen to her while I'm really thinking of a new plot line for a book. I promise that most of the time I am listening.